'I would not marry you should you go down on not one but both knees and beg me humbly to do so.'

'I promise you will never be subjected to any such ludicrous sight, ma'am,' Adam avowed. An amused chuckle drifted back to her, making her insides writhe.

'Don't you dare laugh at me, or go before I have finished speaking,' Sylvie warned him, stamping a dainty shoe. 'I will not have it again. You ran away yesterday, you coward, before I had a chance to say my piece.'

Adam turned about and leaned back on the rusty wrought iron, his arms crossed over his chest. 'You might have lost your innocence.' Deep brown eyes flowed insolently over her body in a way that made Sylvie's face flame. 'But it's not helped to improve you. You're still a tiresome child.'

D1103538

Dear Reader

The Meredith Sisters series was launched with *Wedding Night Revenge*, which charted the scandalous exploits of Rachel, the eldest of Edgar and Gloria Meredith's four beautiful daughters. In the ensuing novel, *The Unknown Wife*, Isabel took her turn to shock polite society.

The third tale featured June, known as the placid Meredith girl. In *A Scandalous Marriage* she proved herself to be an intrepid character, capable of fighting to protect her marriage and those she loves.

The Rake and the Rebel, the final novel in the quartet, gives the youngest Meredith sister a starring role. Silver is a sweet tomboy, principled and passionate. Adam Townsend is a fêted libertine, used to getting what he wants—and he wants Sylvie…let battle commence…

Four young ladies of differing character and interests, but the Meredith sisters are united in their courage and their resolve to win love and happiness. I hope you enjoy reading about how they succeed.

Mary Brendan

THE RAKE AND THE REBEL

Mary Brendan

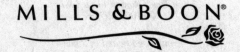

DID YOU PURCHASE THIS BOOK WITHOUT A COVER?

If you did, you should be aware it is **stolen property** as it was reported *unsold and destroyed* by a retailer. Neither the author nor the publisher has received any payment for this book.

All the characters in this book have no existence outside the imagination of the author, and have no relation whatsoever to anyone bearing the same name or names. They are not even distantly inspired by any individual known or unknown to the author, and all the incidents are pure invention.

All Rights Reserved including the right of reproduction in whole or in part in any form. This edition is published by arrangement with Harlequin Enterprises II B.V. The text of this publication or any part thereof may not be reproduced or transmitted in any form or by any means, electronic or mechanical, including photocopying, recording, storage in an information retrieval system, or otherwise, without the written permission of the publisher.

This book is sold subject to the condition that it shall not, by way of trade or otherwise, be lent, resold, hired out or otherwise circulated without the prior consent of the publisher in any form of binding or cover other than that in which it is published and without a similar condition including this condition being imposed on the subsequent purchaser.

MILLS & BOON and MILLS & BOON with the Rose Device are registered trademarks of the publisher.

First published in Great Britain 2005
Harlequin Mills & Boon Limited,
Eton House, 18-24 Paradise Road, Richmond, Surrey TW9 1SR

© Mary Brendan 2005

ISBN 0 263 84388 2

Set in Times Roman 11 on 14¼ pt.
04-1005-59597

Printed and bound in Spain
by Litografia Rosés S.A., Barcelona

Mary Brendan was born in North London but now lives in rural Suffolk. She has always had a fascination with bygone days, and enjoys the research involved in writing historical fiction. When not at her word processor she can be found trying to bring order to a large overgrown garden, or browsing local fairs and junk shops for that elusive bargain.

Recent titles by the same author:

A ROGUISH GENTLEMAN
WEDDING NIGHT REVENGE*
THE UNKNOWN WIFE*
A SCANDALOUS MARRIAGE*

The Meredith Sisters

Look for
THE SILVER SQUIRE
and
A ROGUISH GENTLEMAN
in
The Regency Lords & Ladies Collection
Coming November and December 2005

Prologue

Autumn 1820

'If you think to sweeten me with a brace of pheasant dangled beneath my nose, you may think again!'

Silver Meredith's response to her mother's ingratitude was a saucy smile that widened a quite beautifully generous mouth. From behind her back was whipped further proof of her successful morning's hunting.

'And hare will find more favour with cook than me. Show them to her.'

'I shall,' Silver said, seizing the opportunity to try to escape. She had not managed more than a pace or two when her mother's next utterance arrested her.

'Once you have deposited those corpses in the stillroom, return here, for I still want to speak urgently to you about this evening.' Gloria Meredith cast a determined look on her youngest daughter. At Silver's dejected frown her mother's eyes widened expressively. 'You may scowl, miss, if you want to, but we *are* going to dine at the Robinsons' and *you* are coming, too!' Immediately Mrs Meredith silenced any insubordination by showing her daughter the palm of a weary hand.

Silver angrily paced the corridors of Windrush, her family home, to regain the crisp clean morning air. Wispy blonde tresses were tossed back from cheeks flushed with frustration as she muttered beneath her breath. Soon she was heading for the stable yard.

A stranger might have been scandalised by the sight of a curvaceous young woman striding along with the lissom length of her thighs accentuated by the leather breeches she wore. Perhaps they might have baulked too at a slender-looking shoulder weighted with a hunting rifle. The two men who observed her approach saw nothing unusual.

Edgar Meredith, sensing his youngest daughter's cross mood, pressed on to his younger companion the game he had bagged and, with a mumbled farewell to them both, sought the comfort of his study and a morning snifter.

The gentleman who remained had been removing the saddle from a roan mare. Now he strolled towards the sullen beauty. 'I said you would have to go this evening,' he sighed in defeat.

Silver shook her head in disgust and placed her hands heavily on her hips.

'You must tell them why you don't want to go there,' the young man cried in some agitation. For a fellow of such brawny stature, his voice sounded oddly weak.

'Oh, it doesn't matter,' Silver muttered with a flap of a hand. 'I can deal with the vile bully! If he tries to touch me again, he shall have more than kicks and scratches this time. And some explaining to do to his parents!'

'You must tell your papa what he did.'

'No!' Silver rejected quickly. 'Papa is not well enough to be bothered with it. And you must not say anything to anyone…anyone at all.'

She grabbed her friend's sinewy arm and shook it forcefully as he dropped his eyes away from hers. 'Promise me, John Vance, that you will not say a word,' she demanded.

John simply nodded and returned to the mare. A curry comb began its rhythmic caress over the creature's firm flanks. 'You should have let me deal with him. I'd have milled him good and proper.'

'No! It's what he wants,' Silver fiercely disagreed. 'He wants to provoke you so he has a good excuse to beat you badly this time.'

It was an allusion to a certain incident that made ruddy colour flood John's face. He was abashed at being reminded of an occasion when Hugo Robinson had knocked him unconscious, then kicked him mercilessly while he lay helpless on the ground.

Silver enclosed him in a hug that was unselfconscious and affectionate. 'Have you thought any more about my suggestion—my *perfect* solution to our problems?'

John shrugged himself away, his eyes downcast. The solid leather saddle discarded on the floor was poked with the toe of a boot. Once he had violently shifted that over the dust, the same boot gently turned the lifeless creatures they had bagged. 'It's not right. Your parents would be furious. Even your papa will be angry with you…and me…if we do that. You know everyone will say I'm not good enough for you.'

'It's for me to decide who is good enough for me. I shall choose who I want to marry!' Silver emphasised that with a stamp of a small, booted foot. 'We have been friends since childhood and my parents have never raised objections to that. Once the deed is done, people will accept things. Mama knows I will never settle for a dandified bore. When I made my come out I told her I would sooner be an old maid than get shackled to a prating fool! But if you don't *want* to marry me, well, there is no more to be said on the matter.'

'It's not that,' John said, quickly catching her arm to bring her about to face him.

Silver whirled back, her hair escaping its ribbon to fall about her shoulders like a pearly cape. She gave him a small triumphant smile.

'You know I care for you more than anyone else…even my own kin,' John said emphatically. 'And you're more beautiful than any girl I've ever seen.'

Silver's cheeks turned pink and she flapped a hand. 'You don't have to get beauish with me! We're friends!' She went on to tiptoe to peck his cheek before saying with a glint in her eye, 'But you are right. There will be lectures and objections. But a *fait accompli* will foil refusal. So…we must elope and it is time to start to make plans…'

Chapter One

〜〜〜

Spring 1821

'Get dressed and make ready to leave this fleapit.'

The tall, dark-haired gentleman had spoken dispassionately while surveying rumpled sheets and entangled limbs shocked to paralysis. A thin smile barely lifted one corner of his mouth as he turned on his heel with every intention of quitting the bedchamber. The room was housed in a tavern that was situated an annoying distance from London along the Great North Road. The brunette woman had received the brunt of his flint-eyed contempt. Now she extricated herself from the covers, and her blond lover, and flung herself upright in bed.

'You're so righteous it makes me sick! You've

had more women than I could count, yet you would deny me a little fun! How dare you look at me as though I'm less than dirt beneath your shoe?'

The interloper had stopped and was now lounging against the door through which he had moments before inconspicuously entered the room. He raised his eyes from contemplation of his nails and an indolent look lingered on white breasts swelling at him with each ragged, indignant breath she gulped. The woman preened furiously beneath his lazy gaze.

'I have been greatly inconvenienced by this latest escapade, Theresa. I advise you to curb your tongue. I have far more important things to occupy my time than checking out wretched dives where I might find you fornicating.' His eyes wandered on, prompting her nervous lover to swing his legs over the side of the bed. Swiftly he snatched at his breeches discarded on the floor and jumped into them.

'She's right, you know, Townsend,' the man ground out as he buttoned himself up. 'If you weren't such a blasted hypocrite, I might feel worse about being caught like this.'

'He's not meddling because he cares a jot for himself! He's only concerned for his dear mother's feelings and to protect the family's good name. Hah! What a joke! Rockinghams have always been an infamously horny clan and everyone knows it!'

'It's true my mother dislikes having a whore as a daughter-in-law and who could blame her? Get back to your wife, Sheldon, before I forget that once we were friends and run you through.'

Tobias Sheldon grabbed at his coat and revealed beneath it a stubby horse pistol that had been resting on the same chair. Unconsciously he tested the weapon's weight on a palm.

'If you want to use it…use it,' Adam Townsend invited softly. 'But, to protect both our families from scandal, I would suggest a more discreet meeting. I'll find the misty glade; you may have the choice of weapons.'

Tobias slid a glance at his mistress, who dared and encouraged him with sultry, sparking eyes. With a sheepish look he stuffed the gun in a pocket.

'Very sensible,' Adam drawled with a half-smile. 'She isn't worth the trouble, is she?'

Within a few moments the man's escape was audible as he clattered down the timber treads.

His desertion tightened the woman's mouth into an indignant knot. In frustration she swiped a small, stylish boot from the floor and hurled it. With a lithe sideways step Adam evaded the missile and watched it crash into the door. Proof of her vile temper caused him to elevate one dark brow, and that prompted her to spring from the bed with a feral cry and fly, with curled fingers, straight at him. Strong arms defeated her attempt to scratch his face. The moment her writhing became more sensuous he turned her about, and gave her nude shoulders a little insolent push, so she stumbled towards the bed.

'Get yourself dressed, Theresa. I'll wait below for no more than ten minutes.'

'Ten minutes!' she stormed, flouncing about and striking a pose with her hands on provocatively jutting hips. A theatrical stare slid to the pile of expensive finery heaped on a rustic stool. 'You expect I might make myself decent in that time?'

'Not at all, my dear,' he rejoined lightly. 'I expect ten years might not be adequate. Just put on your clothes and save your sulking for the journey south. Sheldon's gone now, and taken his money with him, so either do as you're told or settle the shot yourself and make your own way home.'

He closed the door, a mirthless chuckle scratching his throat as a thud followed by a vibration in the wood told him both her shoes had been launched and missed their target. A shrill shriek of annoyance prolonged the din, as did some inventive cursing. Having recently gained his father's title unchallenged, he deemed some of it slander. The rest he fairly acknowledged to be valid.

Below in the taproom Adam Townsend, Marquess of Rockingham, got himself a brandy and a chair by the window. He stared out into the gloom and, by the meagre light of an oil lamp, watched Tobias Sheldon conversing with an ostler who had brought round his carriage. Soon the vehicle was swaying away and Adam observed his departure with a subdued sadness. Once he had liked Tobias. Now their friendship had soured because of the slut upstairs. But then Theresa Montague, as she had been before marriage, had a persuasive way about her. He had first-hand experience of that. God, how he wished he had never succumbed to her poisonous charm, for it was through him she was now part of the Rockingham family, and relishing tearing it asunder.

He leaned back in the uncomfortable chair, the rough wood slats spiteful on his spine. Idly he wondered whether to bother finding somewhere cosier to while away the time till Theresa deigned to come below. He knew she would be an hour or more. It was probably her intention to tarry so long that he would be drawn back upstairs to chivvy her. He took out his watch, then stared moodily into the tavern courtyard. It was six-thirty, drizzling, and shrouded in premature gloom. It would be sensible to delay their travel till the morning. In a short while it would be pitch black, and he didn't relish an overnight trip that might necessitate him dealing with desperate highwaymen as well as a nagging harpy. His mouth tightened into a grimace. He had had enough drama for one day and it was a serious temptation to bear the expense of hiring a coach and driver for Theresa's use so he could travel alone, in blissful solitude, in his curricle.

She would be tearful and argumentative at the proposal, but he had a desperate need to be private while his guilt again ravaged his mind. On a sigh he gazed again into the dusk. The brandy tot was on its way to his mouth, but it hovered in space short of its target. A look of profound astonishment cleared the cynicism from his features and fully parted long lashes that had been low over his weary eyes. He turned his head and peered while several long elegant fingers actually cleared a circle on grey, gritty glass through which he might peer. He threw himself back in the chair with a dazed look on his face. Within a moment he was again staring, frowning, striving to convince himself that the young woman to whom he had once proposed was actually outside in the pouring rain, her shimmering hair slicked flat against her scalp. The brandy was emptied into his throat as he stood up.

* * *

Silver ran a finger over the glossy coachwork and the dent between her brows deepened. It was the sort of vehicle that once had impressed her very much. She couldn't be sure the coachwork was black…it might have been a dark shade of green or blue. The light was poor and it was hard to tell, but the impeccably behaved pair in harness seemed familiar. It was the sort of flashy conveyance favoured by gentlemen of the *ton* who liked to appear soigné whilst travelling at full pelt.

Once she had begged to be taken out in a curricle just like this one. The gentleman who owned it had ignored her request, and sometimes that still needled…but rarely, of course, for she never dwelled on the memory…

'Do you still want a ride in it?'

Silver whirled about, jumping a little as though the offer had been bellowed instead of drawled in a seductively soft baritone.

She tilted her head back, while belatedly scrabbling for her bonnet hanging on its strings down her back. Too late she jammed it on her slippery silver-blonde hair as though to conceal her identity. A pair of dark eyes, glinting with warmth and amusement, met her startled wide-eyed stare.

'Lord Malvern…I…er…what are *you* doing

here?' Silver blurted breathlessly, darting an agitated look about.

The mingling of annoyance and accusation in her tone was not lost on Adam. He looked mock-affronted and said, 'I was about to ask you the very same thing, Miss Meredith.' Following her example, he looked around as though to discover with whom she was travelling, for she could not be alone at such an establishment. 'I suppose I should be flattered that you recognised me at all. It has been a while; more than two years, is it not, since…?' The reminiscence remained unfinished and he gave her a long look. 'I think the last conversation we had closed with your wish never to see or speak to me ever again. Must I apologise for putting myself in your way?'

Silver coloured hotly at the soft irony and was glad of the cool mist on her skin and the muted light that camouflaged her high colour. 'I was a deal younger then, sir and…unwisely outspoken at times…'

'And now you are not?' Adam's rueful grin strengthened.

Silver's chin tilted immediately at his mockery. She had been, at sixteen, undeniably naïve and impetuous. She also recalled being rude rather than diplomatic when declining this man's proposal of marriage.

Adam's eyes roved the delicately beautiful face

turned to his. A definite belligerence had skewed her sweet mouth. For all her protestations that her youth had been to blame for her lack of manners two years ago, he rather thought he might get another tongue lashing.

'Are you here with your mother, or one of your sisters?'

Silver swallowed and after a tiny hesitation prevaricated quickly, 'When last we spoke, I was not alone in being unkind. As I recall, you were rude too. You called me an infuriating brat.'

'Ah, well…I, too, was a lot younger then—and unwisely outspoken. Had I not been, I would never have proposed to you at all.'

Silver stared up at him, feeling unaccountably miffed at that. 'I don't believe you. You did want to marry me—' She broke off at his expression and felt herself warming beneath his low-lidded regard. 'I fear you are laughing at me, sir. I'm afraid my temper is always roused when I am mocked. Best that we part this time without rancour. Good evening.' Quickly she made to slip past, heading for the tavern entrance.

'Who are you travelling with? Where are you bound?' The hand on her arm was light, but there was no amusement now in his tone and the query demanded an answer.

A pool of golden light spilling into the dusk made Silver glance nervously at the tavern door. A low oath escaped her as she saw who emerged into the night.

'I fear, Miss Meredith, that you have not changed much at all,' remarked the man closest to her on hearing her muttered expletive.

Silver was barely aware of that wry observation, for her gaze was concentrated on John Vance as he strode the cobbles towards them. She tried to communicate her instructions to him with her wide, expressive eyes. But distance and darkness defeated her and he hastened dutifully on.

'They have a chamber and will prepare us a meal. Who is this?' John burst out in his plain way. He looked at Silver and then at Adam.

Adam regarded the strapping young fellow who seemed to be standing far too close to Miss Meredith for propriety. Perhaps he was a trusted family servant…or perhaps he wasn't, he thought acidly as the fellow took Silver's hand and threaded it through his arm.

'Are we to be introduced?' Adam asked mildly as his eyes narrowed on the handsome newcomer who was holding Silver's hand on his sleeve in a most proprietary fashion.

Silver glared at the ground as though demanding

it open up and swallow her. Why had they not travelled further and broken their journey at a less conspicuous place? Of all the posting houses and taverns situated along the Great North Road, why did this man, of all people, have to be at this very one?

There was nothing for it now but to take the bull by the horns and reveal why she and John were travelling together. A wary glance flicked up at the distinguished gentleman watching her and, for a moment, their eyes tangled in a way that stirred oddly poignant memories.

When last Adam Townsend had stared at her like that she had felt flustered, and that had irritated her. So she had told him so. She had rebuffed Hugo Robinson in much the same way and he had snorted a coarse laugh and said he would show her why he stared. And, to her utter disgust, he had.

Just as she was about to break the expectant quiet with a careful explanation, her travelling companion blurted nervously, 'I am John Vance and this lady is my wife.'

Chapter Two

'Your wife?'

The amused disbelief in Adam's tone caused Silver's head to snap up. 'Yes, I am Mrs Vance. And if you will excuse us both, we are hungry. My husband has bespoken us a hot meal and a chamber.'

'The room is ready and we can eat now if we don't mind dining upstairs,' John advised.

Silver's rash hope that they might now simply escape was soon dashed. Adam silently digested the situation, but his shock was a powerful force that momentarily held them all in a tableau.

'Forgive me for being somewhat tardy in introducing myself. Of course, you do not know who I am. Adam Townsend at your service.' There was the briefest pause before he added, 'Congratula-

tions, Mr Vance, you're a fortunate man to have se-
cured Miss Meredith's affections.'

John grinned and mumbled thanks, then stuck
out a hand.

Without hesitation Adam met that calloused
grip with well-manicured fingers that concealed
surprising strength.

'Good evening, sir,' Silver babbled, and was
soon steering John towards the inn. So fervently did
she wish to quit Adam's overpowering presence
that it was not until they were mounting the rickety
stairs to their chamber that she thought it odd he had
not introduced himself as the Earl of Malvern.

'Damnation!' Silver exploded immediately the
door of their chamber had closed on the servant
who had brought their meal.

John looked uneasily at the willowy figure pac-
ing to and fro across a threadbare rug. It was hard
not to notice that her small hands were curled into
fists that beat at her skirts in time with her steps.
'Come, sit down and eat,' he urged as she continued marching.

'I can't eat! Why in Heaven did we have to
chance upon *him*?'

'Why is chancing upon him any worse than…
than chancing upon others who might know one
or other of us?'

'Oh, it just is!' Silver stormed. But in truth she knew that John was right. It was excruciatingly bad luck to have come face to face with any acquaintance. With many miles between their homes in Hertfordshire and this coaching inn it seemed safe to make a stop. The Great North Road had other hostelries to tempt weary travellers within their doors. The Merediths socialised in polite society. John's parents rarely went out at all, being elderly and burdened with the running of their farm. Silver had thought that the risk of running into anyone who might recognise them at a grubby place such as this was too slim to fret over. She glanced at John as he tucked into a wedge of steak and oyster pie, then upended a tankard. How wrong she was! And what on earth was a peer of the realm doing at such a place? Perhaps Adam had not used his title when introducing himself because he was embarrassed to be found lodging here… Silver dismissed that line of thought. He hardly looked on his uppers. And she imagined hell might freeze over before Adam Townsend was shamefaced.

'Oh, I don't know how you can gorge yourself when this has happened,' Silver said crossly.

John laid down his fork and looked guilty. 'But I don't understand why you are so overset. It must come out that we are married.'

'But not yet! Not before the ceremony has even taken place. We are not halfway to Gretna Green.'

'But you said to tell the landlady that we were already wed.' John looked confused and awkward.

'Yes, I know,' Silver sighed. 'For propriety's sake we must stick to that story while we are in company. A suspicious prig of a landlady might see fit to alert the authorities to any irregularity.'

'So why does it matter if Townsend thinks we are already wed? In a day or two it will be the truth.'

Silver abruptly sat down in the chair opposite John. 'I don't know.' She picked up the fork and poked at the food on her plate. 'I just think… feel… Do you suppose he believed us? He seemed dubious.'

John took one of her fidgety hands between both of his. 'He seemed a regular fellow to me, and well-heeled. How do you know such a toff? Is he a friend of your father's?'

Silver shook her head. 'He is a friend of my brother-in-law William Pemberton. Adam Townsend is the Earl of Malvern. Do you remember when I returned from London after that horrible time when I was kidnapped? Lord Malvern helped William to rescue my sister and me from that blackguard.'

'I do remember you telling me about your brother-in-law's friend.' John nodded, awed. He retrieved his fork and plunged it into his dinner.

'I'm sorry. Eat up,' Silver urged softly. 'The pie will get cold.' She felt guilty now for having been short with John. It was not his fault that fate had frowned on them. Had she not loitered about that fancy curricle Townsend owned, he might never have come across her. Obviously he would keep an eye on such an expensive equipage.

After a few mouthfuls of delicious meat and pastry her hunger won and she set about the meal with gusto. A cup of sweet ruby wine fired her insides and soon she felt a little more relaxed. 'We will leave early in the morning and set on the road. If his lordship does not leave tonight—and I doubt he will in this foul weather and darkness—we will be up and gone before he stirs.'

'I cannot believe that she would do this to us! And in such an underhand, sly way!'

Edgar Meredith wearily raised his sparse-covered head from the comfort of crabbed fingers. 'Our Sylvie has ever been a clever minx,' he said, choosing to call his daughter by the nickname her family often used. 'Did you think she would not plan such a move meticulously?'

'Well, there is no need to sound quite so impressed by it all,' Gloria huffed as she mused on how her youngest daughter had duped them all into being unaware of her absence for almost one whole day. Sylvie had retired to her room yesterday with a headache soon after teatime, saying she did not want to be roused for dinner. By the time the alarm was raised just before noon this morning, and the brief note containing the reason for her absence had been read, screwed into a ball, then retrieved from the floor to be screamed at once more, the runaways had gained a good head start. 'What are you to do about it?'

Edgar slumped back into the wing armchair by the fire. 'What would you have me do about it, my dear? She has not gained her majority, but neither is she a child. If she has set her heart on marrying John Vance, then John Vance she will marry and nothing you or I say or do will make a jot of difference.'

'How can you say that? The match is not suitable!' Gloria shrieked. 'Sylvie is of gentle birth and exceptionally beautiful!'

'And John is of good country stock and very handsome.'

'Yes, but he is…well, a trifle…' Gloria whirled an explanatory hand and shook her head.

'He is a fine young man,' Edgar said quietly.

'John is kind and generous and he adores our daughter. Besides,' he added jovially, 'they will never go hungry, for he can hunt and fish and is a first-class shot.' Seeing that his wife was not amused by his levity, he continued seriously, 'And he has a comfortable living from his grandfather's estate.'

'*A comfortable living?* Sylvie must not end as a farmer's wife!' Gloria shrieked. 'She is destined to marry well. Did she not receive a proposal of marriage from an earl when not turned seventeen? She is more graceful, less fanciful now than she was then. She must socialise in the right circles. She will be inundated with offers…surrounded by suitors…I know it.'

'Has it not occurred to you, Gloria, that perhaps threatening her with such has caused her to run off? Forgive me, my dear, but I think constantly badgering her over returning to town to again endure the marriage mart has prompted her to bolt with a man she at least likes.'

'So it is my fault, is it, that she has absconded with that dimwit?'

Edgar looked cross. 'There are worse things a man can be than slow with his reading and writing.'

Gloria coloured at the subtle rebuke. More diffidently she added, 'Besides, she didn't necessarily need to go to town to find a husband, for there is a perfectly acceptable candidate close by. I'm sure Hugo Robinson likes her very much, yet she will not even go to the Robinsons' to dine. If his mother were not such a particular friend, it would be quite embarrassing forever making excuses for her absence. And *he* is a handsome young man and clever too.'

'As I said, there are worse things a man can be than slow on the uptake,' Edgar said portentously.

'What does that mean?'

'It means that I have heard things about Hugo Robinson that I do not like. Perhaps Sylvie is also aware of the rumours and chooses to avoid him.'

Gloria widened her eyes enquiringly, begging an explanation.

For a moment Edgar remained pensive and quiet. He couldn't be sure all he had heard was correct, and some of it was too indelicate to repeat to a lady, even one's wife. Carefully he told what he knew to be true, for he had witnessed it himself. 'He is a bully. I know he has beaten a couple of the lads in the village, for I was in the vicinity when it occurred. There was no provocation that I could see. Robinson seemed simply intent on showing off to his cronies.'

Gloria looked startled, but was soon waving

away the information with, 'Young men always enjoy a scrap. No doubt he felt silly afterwards to be rolling about at his age. I expect it was a prank.' She cocked her head and said thoughtfully, 'He always seems perfectly charming to me.'

'I'm sure he *is* to you,' Edgar said significantly.

'Oh, you are just making much of it to rile me,' Gloria snapped. 'It won't do talking of what might have been with Hugo! What are we to do to get Sylvie back before her foolishness is known to all and sundry? Are we to again be the target of gossip because we have a daughter who cannot behave?'

'What would you have me do? Shall I summon help from the family to fetch her back?' Edgar was equally anxious that their youngest daughter should not become embroiled in scandal, as had each of her older sisters at some point in their young lives. Those bad times with Rachel, Isabel and June had all come good, so he clung to an optimistic view that his little Sylvie's mishap would not buck the trend. A glance at his wife's agitated countenance caused his confidence to wither. 'If I were a few years younger and fitter, I would set out myself, but now I think I might hinder rather than help.'

'Connor is in Ireland. Étienne is in Suffolk. Only William is close by in town.' Gloria dispiritedly listed the whereabouts of her three sons-in-law.

'Oh, well, I must go then,' Edgar said, quite the martyr.

'No, no, you must not,' Gloria cried. 'The doctor said to live quietly or you might bring on another attack.' She frowned at her husband, who was dramatically supporting himself with the arm of a chair.

'Oh, if she wants to ruin her life, why should I care?' Gloria gestured angrily. 'She has ever been an impetuous, wilful minx. Well, if she thinks to return home for sympathy in a few months when she sees the error of her ways, she may think again. She has made her bed and now she may lie on it!'

'I'm sure she did not want ever to leave home. She never seemed to me a girl with an eye for a husband.'

'All girls want to be married,' Gloria insisted with a jut of her chin. 'It is a natural vocation to find a worthy gentleman who will be kind…and provide nice things, of course.'

'Ah, there we have it. He must have a bankable eligibility above all other considerations. Did you fulfil your vocation in life, Gloria?' Edgar asked softly.

Gloria regarded her faded husband. In truth, it was hard to see in him the dapper young man he once had been. 'I exceeded my expectations,' she told him with a smile. 'I deem myself a fortunate woman.'

'You are being kind, my love,' Edgar said but his pleasure plumped up his sunken chest.

'I suppose it is pointless setting out after them, in any case,' Gloria said with a note of resignation. 'They have been gone too long and she is compromised. Should we manage to bring her back, and the misadventure leak out, then we must make sure that John Vance marries her whether he will or won't.'

'John's parents are no happier than are we, Gloria.' Edgar took a slow march about the room. 'Frank Vance has offered to accompany me should I give chase. He is shakier on his pins than I am. In truth, I think they hold our daughter to blame, even though she is the younger.'

'John is already twenty-two! How can they think that our little Sylvie, who is but eighteen, might be the culprit?'

Edgar gave his wife a wry smile. 'I think we all know who is the instigator in this, Gloria. John worships the ground our Sylvie treads on. It is her idea, you may be sure on it.'

Sylvie stirred to wakefulness as the first flush of dawn warmed her eyelids. She enjoyed that cosy sensation for no more than a few minutes, for her refreshed brain was already retrieving memories she would rather forget.

She struggled upright, keeping the covers tight about her chilly form, and squinted at John snoring softly in the armchair. His chestnut hair was lank and tousled and tumbling over his closed eyes. With his chin dropped on to his chest and his mouth forming a pout, he looked more boyish than usual. As Sylvie regarded her sleeping friend, an odd desire assailed her to know if Adam Townsend dropped that ironic, debonair image when he believed himself unobserved. Perhaps he did, but she was certain he would not look vulnerable, even when unconscious.

Annoyed with herself for pondering on such a triviality, she swung two shapely legs over the side of the bed and padded to the window to peer out. The proof that the dratted man was still close by met her bleary gaze. His smart curricle was still in the open cart lodge, but the beautiful ebony horses had been taken out of harness.

Quality rarely stirred early. Sylvie hoped fervently that Lord Malvern would respect that regime even when put up at such a seedy establishment as this. By the time he greeted the day, she hoped to be some miles away; she had no intention of risking further discussion of her marriage and circumstances.

Quickly turning from the window, she gave John's shoulder a wakening shake. He started and rubbed his eyes.

''Tis time to go, John,' she said urgently. 'Lord Malvern is still here and another meeting with him is best avoided.'

John grunted and sleepily felt about the floor for his boots and began pulling them on.

'I shall make myself presentable while you pay the bill,' Sylvie directed him and drew out her money from a little pouch.

John took what was proffered with one hand whilst the other attempted to straighten his crumpled clothes.

When alone, Sylvie washed, shivering, in the icy water from the pitcher, then put on her warm travelling clothes. The rain had dried on her hair whilst she slept and now angelic pale curls, which resisted severe attempts to flatten them, framed a perfectly oval face. She peered into the spotted mirror on the dressing chest, pushing it this way and that on its hinges as she frowned at her appearance. Large eyes, the grey-blue hue of violent storm clouds, stared back at her. She pinched at her ivory cheeks to try to liven them with a little colour. She did not look her best and was honest enough to acknowledge that that was another reason for avoiding his lordship. With an exasperated huff, she gave the mirror an impatient push. Why worry what he thought on seeing her bedraggled in daylight? But the reason persisted and pricked her pride. His comment, that he regretted asking her to marry him, had sounded sincere despite his smile. And why should that irk? She had regretted it too!

Sylvie's introspection came to an abrupt halt as John opened the door and announced, 'The bill is settled and Mrs Bragg has given us some food to take on the journey.' He held up a small cloth sack, but frowned. 'I think she might have guessed where we are headed. She handed it to me with quite a knowing wink.'

'Well, I suppose we cannot be the only runaway couple who have stopped here presenting themselves as man and wife.' She gave him a rueful smile. It would not occur to John that perhaps the landlady had been generous and given him a wink because he was a strapping goodlooking fellow. With his broad shoulders and bright blue eyes, John attracted female attention. Sylvie had noticed on several occasions some of the village girls about Windrush eyeing him with interest and speculation. When once she'd teased him over it he had looked vague and said he thought she knew she was the only girl he liked. And when he in turn had teased her, asking if she was jealous, it had been her turn to look bemused.

Sylvie took the few coins John had left after paying the landlady and put them away in her purse. 'I shall wait below till you have washed and made ready.' She hesitated at the door. 'But hurry,' she instructed him urgently. 'I do not want Lord Malvern to witness our departure. He might put two and two together if he sees us head north.'

The courtyard was empty and stillness was thick in the frosty air. Sharp breath stung her throat as Sylvie stepped on to icy cobbles. She turned to glance up at the windows set close to mossy thatch. The curtains were closed. The only soul she had seen, besides John, was Mrs Bragg, who had raised a languid hand to her before it was slapped over her yawning mouth.

Sylvie drank in the scent of spring and stretched her arms up over her head. Reassured that their unseen getaway was imminent, she felt brighter than she had last evening when she had retired confused and anxious. The blush on the horizon and the clear, pale sky compounded her optimism that it would be a good day. Her arms were still high, in a salute to serenity, when she froze and stared.

Two men were peering in a decidedly odd manner about the doors of the first stable. First one, then the other, emerged, leading magnificent horses. Sylvie recognised the animals instantly and her heart plummeted. If the black stallions were being brought round, it could only mean that Lord Malvern was preparing to depart, and sooner than they by the look of things. Their hired rig, and the tired old nags that went with it, would take second fiddle to the preparation of his expensive equipage.

She watched the two men draw closer. They were both still darting glances about and, as Sylvie observed them signalling to one another, and leaning close to whisper, she realised they looked different to the stablemen she had briefly seen last evening when they arrived.

One of these fellows had a scarf tied about his greasy-looking dark hair and the other had a gold hoop through an ear. They had not spotted her and, as she observed their stealthy approach, she noticed that the leading horse seemed jumpy and was being tightly reined in so a hand could clamp over its muzzle. Sylvie felt a combination of trepidation and indignation clench her stomach. They were villains intent on stealing Adam Townsend's horses! Her suspicions were confirmed when the fine animals were led away from the courtyard and the curricle, and towards the spinney beyond the well. The further they got the faster their gait became. Soon both men and beasts would be hidden from view.

To raise the alarm would draw unwanted attention to her and John, yet her conscience would not allow her to do nothing. Drawing in a lungful of breath, and a sigh of resignation, she yelled, 'Stop, thief!'

Chapter Three

The ruffian sporting the colourful headgear was startled on hearing Sylvie's bellow. The sight of her slight figure, cloak flying out behind her, racing towards him caused him to lose his grip on the reins and the animal slipped from his restraint. Now she was closer, Sylvie could see that the hapless chap was the younger of the two men by some years. He lunged clumsily at the horse, trying to recapture it, but hooves flailing close to his head made him crouch and scuttle away.

Sylvie retreated a bit on receiving twin menacing glares. But for the proximity of the inn, and the chance of being caught, she was sure they would have come after her for disrupting their plan. She was still close enough to hear them argue in an unintelligible tongue and to see the pair push and punch at each other. She guessed that neither wanted the blame for their robbery going awry. The felon in possession of a mount sprang lithely on to the animal's bare back. In between dealing slaps to his colleague he helped hoist him up to sit behind. Belligerent eyes were again turned on her as they used their knees to sufficiently tame the animal and send it galloping towards the trees.

Sylvie sped back the way she had come, waving wildly at the landlady who had stationed herself in the kitchen doorway, her jaw dropped on her chest.

'Mrs Bragg! Summon help! Thieves!' Sylvie commanded urgently when she had regained her breath. The woman finally conquered her daze and wobbled into life. Within seconds a commotion could be heard inside. Windows in the eaves were pushed open as some fellows bawled for quiet and others to know what in damnation was going on. Sylvie grimaced apology, her shoulders up against her ears to protect them from the voluble selection of oaths.

John was the first to appear in the courtyard. He hurried towards her. Her portmanteau was dropped at her feet as he listened to her gulped account of what she had witnessed. Before she could conclude the tale Adam Townsend appeared.

A linen shirt was bunched in one of Adam's

fists rather than protecting his torso from the early morning chill. Sylvie had only ever seen this man immaculately attired and for some reason observing him semi-naked caused her narration to cease mid-flow and an odd feeling to tingle through her.

She had seen John in a similar state of undress, lots of times, during the many hot summers they had shared. Her intended had an athletic build and well-muscled arms that rivalled the physique from which her eyes seemed unwilling to detach. She had admired John's shape without feeling like this. She quickly turned away, annoyed with herself, for she could sense a blush seeping into her cheeks. No man, on finding he was being robbed whilst he slept, would tarry to bother with sensibility, even one as refined as Lord Malvern.

Adam strode towards them, a low imprecation bursting from lips that were stretched thin against his teeth. The stolen horse was disappearing into the spinney; the other was being led, snorting, towards its master by a stable-hand.

Adam immediately started to soothe the animal, fondling it gently as it nuzzled his palm. He then looked at the boy with sheer wrathful disgust. 'Was it too much to ask that you care properly for them for the guinea I gave you?'

The young man coloured miserably and stifled

a nervous sob. 'I…I'm real sorry, your lordship. I…I fell asleep…' He withdrew the glinting coin he had been given and gingerly tendered it.

As Adam thrust an arm into his shirt the boy ducked and cringed as he saw a fist coming his way. He obviously anticipated a blow for his negligence. Adam stared at him and then, with his eyes raised heavenward in exasperation, walked away to shove another brown forearm into white lawn. He looked back at the lad. 'If you want to keep that money, you can make yourself useful and assist in getting him back.'

By the time Sylvie's unblinking gaze had reached the top button, along with his long nimble fingers, she was aware that his lordship's eyes harboured amusement in their sultry depths. It was in the ensuing long moment as their eyes entwined that she became aware, properly aware, of how he looked.

Yesterday, when meeting him in evening gloom, she had recognised him immediately simply from his voice and that potent air of authority he exuded. Yet two years ago she had not taken much notice of his features. Oh, she had digested his overall appearance: that he was a handsome imposing gentleman. But what had really absorbed her was inveigling for a ride in his flash curricle, so she could appear as grown up and fashionable as her older sisters. Now she noticed individual features: his nose was distinctly bridged and the colour of his eyes odd. The shade reminded her of seaweed she once had seen glittering on the beach at Lyme Regis. Brown or green could equally be used to describe it. His face was thin, sharp about the jaw, and his skin held a healthy golden tan. Her complexion was similarly glowing. Her mother was always scolding her for not shading her features with a hat when she was out in the air with her papa and John. The only aspect of his looks that had made an impression on her when she was sixteen was his raven hair. Once, when he had been seated and she was standing by his side, she had taken an interested peer at the few silver strands in amongst the black at his temples. She could recall coming to the conclusion that he must be quite old. Two years had passed; oddly, he didn't now look *so* old. Her inspection had fallen to a firm, moulded mouth and she blinked as it suddenly spoke to her.

'My apologies, ma'am, for my shocking state this morning. I must offer you my thanks too. I hear from Mrs Bragg that, but for your timely intervention, I would have lost both animals.'

Sylvie made a modest gesture, then said gruffly, 'I'm sorry I was not brave enough to try and stop them making off.'

'I think you are extremely brave to even consider doing so, Mrs Vance,' Adam said gently.

Her fascination with his beautifully stern features was abruptly curtailed as she heard him address her for the second time as a married woman. She immediately flicked an index finger at the trees as though expecting he might immediately set to and do as she suggested. 'If you go now, you might still catch them.' For just a short while this new drama had overshadowed a more personal predicament. Now she was reminded of the urgent necessity to set on the road to Scotland and dispense with the lie she and John had concocted for propriety's sake.

'I'll help you get him back, too, if you like,' John suddenly volunteered.

Sylvie stiffened, cursing inwardly at John's simple thoughtlessness. She slid a warning glance at him. He blithely smiled, so she glared until he comprehended her silent instruction and his affable expression crumpled. 'Unfortunately, we must be on our way,' Sylvie said as sweetly as her mood would allow.

'Oh…yes…we must be on our way,' John mumbled while rubbing at his unshaven chin and giving Adam a shy yet assessing look. He didn't seem like a fellow who really needed help from anyone to recover what was his, John concluded.

Adam's expression grew ever more sardonic as he looked from one to the other of them and sensed the tension. 'It's too early in the morning to be tracking felons. After I've had breakfast I'll summon the energy…and the authorities. But thank you both for your concern. I am especially grateful to you, Mrs Vance, for raising the alarm.'

Sylvie sensed herself flinch at another reference to her spurious status.

'You must allow me to repay you in some small way. Will you both take breakfast with me in the Braggs' back parlour?'

'Thank you, sir, for your generosity, but we must be going immediately.'

Sylvie slipped a hand through John's arm and gave it a subtle tug. A clatter in the kitchen was soon followed by the piquancy of brewing coffee and frying bacon, and the crisp air seemed to mellow with the wonderful aroma. She knew John might find it difficult to refuse another invitation to take a hot meal before they set out for she had just heard his stomach grumble that it needed to be fed.

'Where are you headed? Home?' Adam asked conversationally. 'And where is that exactly?'

Sylvie mumbled, 'Hertfordshire', then turned a shoulder, hoping to deter any further questions.

She noticed that a crowd had gathered to pick over the bones of the drama. People, some still in their nightclothes, were pointing towards them and obviously regaling each other with their own version of events. At that moment Sylvie sensed they were being observed from another direction and tipped back her head.

A woman was leaning out of a bedchamber window directly above, and it was quite obvious that she was in the process of eavesdropping on their conversation. She was pretty although her mouth was at a sulky slant. Her dressing gown seemed to have been casually dragged about her shoulders and her lush white bosom spilled on to her wrists as she leaned over the sill. Despite her state of undress, she had an air of haughty confidence about her as she boldly returned Sylvie's stare.

Sylvie noticed that Adam was also aware they were being closely observed. His eyes raised and his mouth tightened. That subtle sign of his displeasure was enough to make the brunette suddenly duck out of sight. The window was then slammed with a force that threatened to shatter the panes and shower them all with glass.

From being moments ago impatient to be gone, Sylvie now found herself prey to a vulgar curiosity. Who was the sullen woman and how had she managed to so easily annoy Lord Malvern? Were they travelling together? Two years ago she might have given way to her inquisitiveness and simply asked him, for she could not deny she had once been outrageously impertinent with this man. He had quietly tolerated her unseemly behaviour and answered her audacious questions. Thus, at sixteen, she had learned from a stranger that demireps were women of dubious reputation with whom he sometimes kept company. It was the sum of her worldly education that year; her embarrassed father had then succeeded in banning her from the gentlemen's presence. Since then she had learned more of the ways of men, not least to be cautious in her dealings with them...

Adam was watching the emotions that flitted over her flawless face. She had lost innocence since last they met, that was obvious. Two years ago she would have simply pointed and demanded to know who that woman was. Now she thought she knew who Theresa was. She thought he was holed up in this dump with a mistress. He wasn't sure why he felt injured that she suspected he was sordid enough to conduct a tryst in such paltry surroundings.

His indignation was lost to his obsession with knowing why this unique child had married a man who was blatantly her inferior. Not that John Vance was ugly or unpleasant. In fact, from their very brief acquaintance, he had gathered that John Vance was possibly too docile and handsome for his own good. He would hazard a guess he was certainly not the sharpest tool in the box. Nevertheless, he had no reason at all to dislike him…yet he feared he did. And he refused to investigate why that should be.

'Pardon me, m'lord.' Mrs Bragg had sidled unseen up to the trio and quivered into a deep curtsy. 'Lady Townsend says as she'd like to speak to you direct, like…' The landlady's lowered eyes shot sideways, indicating the tavern.

For a moment Sylvie was sure he was going to send back a snarled response. Instead a look of pure irritation tautened his features. 'Excuse me just a moment.' It was gritted out as he executed a small bow. In a moment he was striding away towards the tavern.

So stunned was Sylvie by the idea that the brunette was his wife that for some moments she was unaware that Mrs Bragg was eyeing her unadorned wedding finger. Quickly she withdrew her hand from John's arm and thrust it into her cloak pocket.

'Lady Townsend? His lordship is travelling with

his wife?' she asked, hoping to distract her with a disarming smile and a little gossip.

A crafty laugh preceded, 'Whatever she calls herself, I doubt *that* lady is married to that gentleman any more than…' Mrs Bragg pursed her lips, while knowingly rolling her eyes. She whispered, 'Keep wrapped up in that cloak 'cos it's bitter cold where you're going.'

Sylvie darted a look at John, but the sly hint that the game was up as far as the landlady was concerned seemed to have escaped him. 'We ought be getting along,' Sylvie said and gave John a dig in the ribs. She realised it would be better to tackle Mrs Bragg alone to find out what she knew. John was prone to saying the wrong thing and could make matters worse.

'I'll get the rig made ready,' John said and strode purposefully towards the stables.

Mrs Bragg grinned and nodded, a glint in her eye. 'I'm a romantic soul meself. Me 'n Mr Bragg was sweethearts a long while afore we wed.'

Further pretence seemed futile, but it was imperative that the landlady didn't convey her astute suspicions to anyone else, especially to her noble guest. 'You've guessed we are travelling to Gretna Green.'

The landlady leaned close to pat Sylvie's arm. 'Don't fret about me, miss. I got here an inn to run, not a mission. We sees all sorts stopping over at the George 'n Dragon. I can tell you're a *proper* young lady, not like the sort upstairs—all airs and graces and alleycat ways. I hope it goes right for you.'

Sylvie managed a faint smile and disengaged her arm. 'Thank you. But I must ask you a favour, Mrs Bragg, for I…we…find ourselves in an awkward situation. I must beg you not to reveal to anyone what you have guessed. That gentleman is acquainted with my family and could…well, if he knew that I am not yet in fact Mrs Vance, I'm *sure* he would feel obliged to take me home.'

Mrs Bragg slapped a fat finger against her nose and proceeded to tap at it. 'Me lips are sealed. I'll tell him nothin' even if he asks. Lucky for you his lordship's got a right job on his hands getting back his horse and keeping that brazen hussy in order. Right temper she's got. I heard her hollering! Anyhow, he's no right to go a-sermonising to you young folk. He's not the gent she arrived with, you know. T'other one took off just after his lordship arrived.'

As Sylvie's expression transformed from disbelief to disgust, Mrs Bragg coughed and muttered, 'Well, enough of them and what they're up to. I hope you know what you're up to. You've got a fine strong lad there. He's a looker, but not brash with his charm like some young bucks as know all

they have to do is crook a finger to get the girls running.' Mrs Bragg added on a wise nod, 'Handsome couple you make. I expect your kin'll come
round once they're dandling bonny grandsons on
their knees. But be sure you know what you're
doin', for life's hard at the best of times without
your family turnin' its back on you.' She nodded
at John, who was steering the gig towards them
with a contented smile.

'Go on; off you go, then, and be lucky!'

'What is it?' John asked quietly. They had barely
spoken two words together in as many miles.

At the recommencement of their journey north
they had been discussing the commotion that had
taken place at the inn and debating whether or not
his lordship would be successful in retrieving his
horse. Now there was no more to say on the subject and their own thrilling predicament could no
longer be ignored.

Sylvie gave John a vague smile, but an unconscious sigh escaped as she pulled the travelling rug
tighter about her.

'Are you worried that Mrs Bragg will betray us
after all? Do you think Townsend might find out
we are runaways and come after us?'

'No…well she might have told him… Oh, I

don't know!' Sylvie cried. Suddenly the roiling thoughts that were battering her mind would no longer be contained. She flung herself round on the seat and mimicked the landlady's parting words to them. '*Be lucky!* 'Tis not luck we need, but common sense! Why did I overlook such a silly thing? Had she seen a ring on my finger she would have been none the wiser to any of it, I'm sure. Why did I pack away the ring?'

'But you said to keep our valuables hidden in case we were set upon by highwaymen,' John reminded her. 'And you were right,' he praised her. 'Those gypsies are in the neighbourhood.' He took a swift, nervous look about.

'Are you thinking they might come after us?' Sylvie asked. She recalled how resentful they had looked that she had deprived them of the other valuable stallion. She frowned and felt beneath the travelling rug for the gun.

She tapped John's leg with it, hoping to comfort him. 'We have this and must use it if need be. Cowards don't like it if you stand up to them. They will skulk away if challenged.'

John simply frowned and, flicking the reins, urged the elderly mares to a faster trot.

'Do you think Adam Townsend noticed I had no wedding ring?'

John shook his head. 'It was dark when we met him last night and this morning it was all chaos. He seemed more concerned for his horses than anything else.'

Sylvie grimaced at that. Personally, she thought his lordship had been quite cavalier in his attitude to losing the fine animal. What *had* seemed to greatly annoy him was the appearance at the window of the brunette. Sylvie had felt quite sad to learn from the landlady that Adam was debauched enough to share his paramour with another man for, before he had spoiled things and asked her to marry him, she had thought him quite the hero two years ago. She slid John a look. Now she had another hero.

He *was* a hero, she impressed on herself. For her sake he had conquered his misgivings about risking an elopement. He was an only child, and the apple of his elderly parents' eyes, yet he had bravely lied to them because she had said he must. On his return as a married man perhaps they might be estranged. Yet he was doing it for her. She ought be grateful…

Sylvie fell back against the meagre comfort offered by the squabs and studied John's profile. He was as handsome a hero as any woman could want. She watched his calloused fingers on the reins and decided she liked his hands. He might not be high-born or wealthy but, compared to vile Hugo Robinson, who was both, John was a perfect gentleman.

Having convinced herself that all was as it should be, Sylvie suddenly said in a quiet voice, 'I think we should return home.'

Chapter Four

'For goodness' sake, leave her be!'

'*Leave her be?*' Mrs Meredith choked, outraged that such a course of action should even be considered. But she came away from the parlour door through which she had been on the point of speeding to again find and castigate their youngest daughter. 'The selfish chit needs horsewhipping for what she has done to us!'

'Hush, Gloria, you know you do not mean that. Hush now or she will hear you…'

'I hope she *does* hear,' Gloria gritted past the wet cotton scrunched into a ball and pressed to her mouth. 'She should suffer as I have. For her to elope was bad enough. For her to return home unwed after two days and one night in the company of a man is…diabolically indecent behaviour!' The sodden hanky was scrubbed at her red eyes.

'She has already admitted as much and apologised for it,' came Edgar's gentle reminder. He ambled the carpet to try and enclose his distraught wife in an embrace. Her elbows kept him at bay so he simply patted at a hunched shoulder whilst crooning, 'There…there…it is not so bad, you'll see.'

'He must marry her or she is ruined,' Gloria gurgled. 'Make him marry her!'

'It is not John's fault it came to nought, Sylvie has said so.'

'Well, make *her* marry *him,* then!'

'She will not marry anyone.' Edgar's tone was now brusque; he was tired of repeating himself and impatient with his wife for refusing to be consoled. 'First you did not want her gone; now you do not want her back. There is no reason to fret so, Gloria. She is not ruined. I know it was silly of her to want to elope, but who knows about her jaunt? The Vances will say nothing. They would not want John accused of being a wicked philanderer and neither would I. That boy has his heart in the right place, and she might do worse than marry him.'

'Well, make her do it!'

Edgar supplicated at the ceiling with eyes and hands.

'You know Susannah Robinson was here yesterday. You know I had to lie and say that Sylvie was indisposed in her room when in fact she was not even in the house.'

'You did very well, m'dear,' Edgar praised. 'I noticed your friend didn't suspect a thing.'

'You think I ought be proud that my daughter has made of me a liar?'

'I'm sorry, Mama. If I could undo it all I would…'

The husky apology was spoken from the doorway, causing Mr and Mrs Meredith to twist towards it. Before Gloria could launch a tirade, her husband held out his arms. 'You are a bad girl, but I'm glad you are home. Come and give your old papa a hug.'

Sylvie flew over the rug and into his embrace, burying her dainty features against a stout neck. Edgar's weary fingers comfortingly rubbed his daughter's slender back, then picked strands of silver hair from her face so he could dry her tears. 'Come now, my dear, no more waterworks; my shirt is damp.'

A little sob of laughter bubbled close to Edgar's ear. Sylvie pecked her father on the cheek before approaching her mother and giving her a mournful little smile.

She had arrived home yesterday evening just as her parents were retiring for the night. With pleas of exhaustion interspersing her replies to her mother's hysterical demands, she had managed to delay an inquisition. Now she knew she must give a full account of her foolish escapade.

Gloria pursed her lips and gave Edgar a fleeting glare. 'You need not think I am to be so easily appeased, miss,' she announced strictly. 'Doe eyes count for nought as far as I am concerned. Your behaviour has been appalling…'

'And selfish and idiotic and illogical…I know that now, Mama,' Sylvie said softly. 'And I am truly sorry for it. I am more ashamed than you know. Not only have I hurt you, but John and his parents too.'

'I want to know everything that has gone on. *Everything*, do you hear me? How could that John Vance have let you persuade him to be a party to such folly? He is older than you. He is of good family and should act accordingly.'

'The fellow was receiving just such a homily when I saw him this morning,' Edgar intervened while dwelling on a mental picture he had of John sitting with his head dropped in his hands, his father bombarding him with wrathful remarks.

Edgar had sensed he was not welcome, despite

the fact he had visited them to be generous. He had wanted to let the Vances know that he would not be making accusations of seduction or abduction, either to them or to the authorities. He had always liked John; he still did like him, yet he knew proper accord between the two families was lost.

'I made John agree to elope against his better judgement. It is not his fault that we returned unwed. I insisted he bring me home. He should not take the blame for any of it.'

'I'll be the judge of that,' Gloria interrupted pithily, 'when I know exactly what went on between the two of you.'

'We shared a chamber,' Sylvie quietly admitted. 'It was the only one that was available at the George and Dragon. John took the armchair and allowed me the bed. He acted with kindness and gentlemanly respect towards me at all times.'

Gloria's complexion whitened. 'You actually slept together in the same room?' she whispered, aghast.

'Would you rather they had observed etiquette and perished from the cold in that gig?' Edgar interjected. 'I think I'm glad they opted for comfort and safety.' Whilst his wife was recovering from that ironic observation, assisted by her salts, he added briskly, 'The whole affair must now be put aside. Obvious discord between us is sure to engender inquisitiveness. That is when trouble will really start.'

A peek from beneath her lashes informed Sylvie her mother was swayed by that argument. The vinaigrette was no longer being wafted; the top was being firmly replaced. Sylvie wanted to hug her papa again for his sweet mediation. But there was wisdom as well as affection in what he was trying to do. If her aborted elopement became common knowledge, her reputation would be irreparably sullied.

The knowledge that John was suffering too made her feel hot with shame. Yet she had always known they must both return to face their parents' wrath. Slowly she volunteered, 'I think I ought write to Mr and Mrs Vance and just explain…'

'Leave well enough alone, my dear,' Edgar said quietly. 'Let John sort this out with his kin in his own way or you will make the boy look ridiculous. I forget, he is not a boy, is he?' Edgar muttered to himself. 'I'm sure the Vances know you can twist him about your little finger, Sylvie. They will not relish having it rubbed in.'

'I suppose this shocking business should not have come as *that* much of a surprise,' Gloria intoned as she cast a sceptical eye on her demure daughter. 'All three of your sisters have caused a stir at some time in their lives. Why would we escape a catastrophe with you? Thank Heavens your crime was not witnessed by anyone we know.' Gloria relinquished her martyred air to send an astute look towards her daughter. 'You saw and spoke only to strangers, isn't that so?'

Sylvie had been dreading this moment. No more lies! She must not compound the deceit! Such were the good intentions rotating in her mind. But equally she could not bear to be totally honest and say that, on the contrary, her disgrace had been observed by one of society's most distinguished personages. If she were to admit that not only had she seen Adam Townsend but lied to him too, her mother would possibly expire on the spot and her papa would be sure to withdraw his leniency. 'We stopped only the once: at the George and Dragon. I'm confident nobody who was there would betray us, Mama,' she slowly prevaricated. 'And John's parents will, naturally, keep this secret.'

'And when we see Susannah Robinson, as we shall at the weekend when we dine at Rivendale,' Gloria instructed with a narrow-eyed glower daring her daughter's insubordination, 'remember that you have been laid low with a cold. You must make sure you mention it several times.'

Sylvie frowned on learning that news. It appeared a meeting with Hugo Robinson was imminent. After a moment she nodded dutifully and smoothed her stylish skirts. She had dressed today to please her mother. Her morning gown was of sky-blue muslin sprigged with cream rosebuds. With her hands clasped in front of her and her pearly head bowed, she looked beautifully angelic.

Gloria cocked a cynical eyebrow at the vision of loveliness that was her tomboy daughter. 'I must say it's nice to see you dressed in something pretty instead of those dreadful breeches you normally wear.'

Sylvie gave a small smile. 'Papa and I will not go out till this afternoon…'

Edgar gestured a negative to that comment behind his wife's back. On guessing his meaning, Sylvie wrinkled her nose. 'Or perhaps we might not ride today; it looks to be coming on to rain.'

'Perhaps you might not indeed! You are banned from such exploits forthwith. I have told your father it is high time you acted like a well-bred young lady instead of a hoyden. There will be no more dressing and acting like a stable lad. Perhaps June can talk some sense into you when she gets here. I must say, although she got embroiled in a scandal too, it was not at all her fault.'

'June is coming? And William?' Sylvie felt her spirits soaring at that welcome news.

'We received her letter the morning you disappeared. It was every sort of chaos that day, I can tell you,' Gloria grumbled. '*She* had given us little notice of her intention to come and stay and you had given us no notice at all of your intention to run off.'

Sylvie hugged her mother before she could raise her defences. She kissed her cool cheek. 'I shall help the servants get the guest chambers ready. She *is* bringing Jacob?' Sylvie demanded. She adored all her nieces and nephews, but little Jacob, with his tiny toothy giggle and his flaxen curls, held a special place in her heart. She was fond of June's husband too. William Pemberton was a fine gentleman who was universally liked. Her sunny smile clouded as she recalled just who was her brother-in-law's particular friend. She knew she must soon make discreet contact with that very person in order to meekly make a confession…

'What I do not understand is why, having found the audacity to go, you then turned around and came back.'

June Pemberton was snugly ensconced in the little armchair situated in the window embrasure in Sylvie's bedroom. On one of her fragile shoulders rested the rosy round cheek of a drowsing infant. A small hand drew slow rhythmic circles on the boy's plump back, but her wide amber eyes, fixed on her younger sister's face, displayed a zealous interest in their conversation.

Sylvie shrugged and small white teeth sank into her bottom lip.

'You must know why you changed your mind,' June probed. 'Did you and John argue?'

Sylvie shook her head. 'I'm not sure why…a pricking conscience perhaps. Carrying on just no longer seemed…right.' And that was the truth, she realised. There had been no sudden revelation, no momentous decision over which to agonise. An irrepressible sense of unease had simply solidified into words that had slipped off her tongue. Even when she had seen the hurt mingle with bewilderment in John's eyes, she had remained adamant they must abort their plans.

Having spent several months in the planning of it all, having been the one to convince John that it would all come right, he had had good reason to be angry with her for abruptly turning tail. In an odd way she had hoped he would display disappointment…and dominance. It might have turned out differently if, for once, *he* had told *her* what they ought do. But he had simply waited while she decided their futures.

The lie she had told Adam Townsend had not after all been validated and now she must bear the consequences of that terrible deceit. He shared mutual acquaintances with her brother-in-law and should a mention be made of *Mrs John Vance*… A small scowl marred Sylvie's features as she dwelled on the excruciating bad luck they'd had in running into him at all. Had he not been at the tavern, perhaps her plan to become Mrs John Vance would not have been disrupted, for it was there that misgivings had started to assail her.

Sylvie held out her arms to receive her nephew. His mother obligingly handed him over. A small warm head burrowed close to her ear and Sylvie angled her cheek to the sweet sighing breath on her skin. 'He is quite a weight. And much grown in length.' One of her hands cupped curled baby toes.

June was undeterred by her sister's diversionary tactics. 'Something is wrong; oh, I don't mean what has happened with John Vance, although that wasn't right, of course. There's something else. My wicked little Sylvie is missing. You seem different; quite subdued.'

Sylvie sent June a slanted smile. 'It is humility.

I feel a fool for causing all this trouble. I expect it will pass and I shall be a nuisance again.'

'Don't joke! If you won't tell me why you cried off eloping, perhaps you'll tell me why you wanted to marry John Vance in the first place.' On seeing Sylvie's proudly tilting chin, June quickly expanded, 'Oh, I do like him, even if he is a mite…' She hesitated, realising tact was still lacking from her observations. Carefully she said, 'I know he has always been a great friend of yours, but I didn't imagine that you thought of him romantically.'

'I don't.' Sylvie readily dismissed that notion, causing an arch look to wing her sister's eyebrows close to a fringe of fair curls. Sylvie gestured impatiently without missing a single comforting stroke to the child in her arms. 'Oh, Mama has been badgering me again about netting a husband. If I must spend the rest of my days with a man, it's best I choose one I at least like.'

'How do you know there are *not* other gentlemen you might also like? If you socialised in the right circles, you might meet some of them.'

'I don't want to alarm you, June, but you are starting to sound distinctly like one of our parents,' Sylvie mockingly chided. 'Besides, I have now submitted to her browbeating. I have agreed to be dragged off with the rest of you to the Robinsons' soirée.'

* * *

'Why…they are not at home, my lord.' The butler gave the eminent gentleman a deeply respectful bow that was followed by a smile of welcome. 'But do please come in, if you would care to, and I shall find some refreshment.'

Adam Townsend did indeed step over the threshold of Grove House in St James's Square, not for sustenance, but for information. With a perfunctory quirk of a smile responding to the manservant's hospitality, he looked right and left in the vestibule as though still vainly hoping to locate his friend. He had arrived unexpectedly, thereby risking that the Pembertons would be out, yet he felt unaccountably disappointed to find it so. He was deprived of satisfying what he acknowledged was an uncouth curiosity. Prepared to loiter if necessary, he enquired, 'Are Mr and Mrs Pemberton due to return soon?'

'In a fortnight, my lord. They have gone yesterday into Hertfordshire to see Mrs Pemberton's family.'

The butler watched a pair of earth-coloured eyes stare straight ahead and a wide brow pensively furrow. He liked this man despite his notoriety as a licentious scoundrel. His master, William Pemberton, was a gentleman of impeccable taste and manners. If he chose the Marquess of Rockingham to be his best friend, then the butler knew that he was in the presence of integrity no matter what the gossips said. 'Would you like some tea, my lord? Or a drink of something cold?' he hastily amended his offer. His lordship might be a fine fellow, but the butler was reasonably sure he took his beverages strong.

'Thank you, no,' Adam said as he strolled back towards the door. 'Remind me again where Mrs Pemberton's family live in Hertfordshire. I have an inkling that the estate is towards the east of the county.'

'That is correct, my lord. Windrush is situated close to the Essex boundary. Fine countryside it is, too, by all accounts.'

Having taken his leave and descended the stone steps to his vehicle, Adam loitered by the kerb, staring casually up and down the street while he struggled to control a needling frustration. He was allowing a random discovery to become disproportionately important, yet curbing his impertinence and getting along with his own business seemed impossible. His irritation escalated with the realisation that he was deemed to be a master of nonchalance, yet here he was, displaying a vulgar inquisitiveness about a marriage that would put a hardened town tabby to the blush. A dry chuckle erupted, causing a young lady promenading with her friend to turn and give him an interested peek. His mocking salute transformed her coquettishness to indignation and she tossed her head around. Indeed, there was nothing amusing in any of it, he decided soberly as he jumped aboard his curricle. His behaviour was nothing short of ludicrous.

Having glowered at the sleek flanks of his docile horses for some moments, he finally grabbed the reins and urged them to a trot. Thoughts rotated in his mind. He could forget all about Mr and Mrs John Vance…or he could find reasons to further indulge this obsession by transferring himself to Hertfordshire. He certainly had a valid excuse to catch up with William and June Pemberton as soon as possible.

Recently Adam had received a letter from the couple regarding the christening of their firstborn. Had he not been sidetracked by Theresa again stirring up family unrest, he would have days ago dealt with his important post. His secretary was constantly nagging him to dedicate a few minutes a week to his correspondence so he could appear to be running an efficient diary. Thus it was high time that the Marquess of Rockingham conveyed to the proud parents of Jacob Pemberton that he would deem it a privilege to be the boy's godfather.

He grinned to himself and sprang the horses as soon as the road ahead was clear. If that was not enough reason to take him into Hertfordshire, he could find another. As he recalled, Sir Anthony Robinson lived in that direction. He had not seen that fine old chap for some while, for Sir Anthony had been too frail to attend his father's funeral. Indeed, it was high time too that the new Marquess of Rockingham went to pay his respects to a man who had been a close friend to his predecessor, and also happened to be his godfather. Should he happen upon Mrs John Vance while he was in the vicinity of Windrush, then he could convey his renewed thanks to her. Her early warning of the theft at the George and Dragon had certainly been instrumental in him recovering his horse.

Adam quirked a smile on realising he had convinced himself that a sojourn in the country was not an indulgence, but a necessity. Whether it would prove a wise decision, he was not so sure. Since that angelic chit had sent him away, never to return, he could have sworn he had not given her more than a cursory thought. It seemed odd that, now she was married, he could not get Silver Meredith out of his mind.

Chapter Five

'**Y**ou will never guess who is coming to see us!'

The pink taffeta Sylvie had been holding out and regarding with apathy was dropped on to the bed to join a mound of similarly discarded gowns. Choosing a suitable ensemble in which to go to the Robinsons' soirée was a tedious chore she gladly relinquished to hear her sister's news.

June's amber eyes were shiny with excitement. 'This note just arrived for William from the Marquess of Rockingham.' She waved a parchment at Sylvie, simultaneously settling little Jacob on his bottom in the middle of the mattress. 'He is lodging locally and has asked if he may visit tomorrow afternoon. He wants to come and see his future godchild.'

Sylvie frowned; she had never before heard her

sister and brother-in-law speak of any such person and she was acquainted with their close friends. She glanced at the little boy wobbling on the quilt. A rattle was waved at her before the baby jammed it again between tiny, dribbling lips. Sylvie was warmed by a surge of affection for her darling nephew and she quizzed rather impertinently, 'I hope you know this person well. Is he suitable?'

'I know him very well, and think him eminently suitable. You know him too. Ah, you don't recognise his title. Of course you would not, for his father died just last winter and he has never been one for flaunting his ancestry.'

June took Sylvie's hands and pulled her down to sit beside her on the bed for a chat. '*You* know him as the Earl of Malvern or plain Mr Townsend. He has been a good friend of William's for a very long time. We would not choose him simply because he is rich and influential.'

June's enthusiasm for her son's prospective godparent continued, but went unheard by Sylvie. For just a moment longer her stunned smile clung to her full lips. Then the awful news penetrated her mind and she audibly gulped: Adam Townsend was the Marquess of Rockingham! He was coming here tomorrow afternoon to visit them! Even if she took flight to avoid him, polite conversation

over the teacups was bound to turn to a recent
chance meeting he'd had with the Merediths'
youngest daughter…*Mrs John Vance*. He might
amiably recount the minor drama that had un-
folded at a hostelry on the Great North Road con-
cerning the theft of one of his horses… Sylvie felt
the blood drain from her cheeks and a ball of lead
drop to her stomach.

Impolitely she plucked the letter from her sister's fingers and began scanning it for vital clues.
'Where in the village is he staying?' she demanded
in a low breath as her eyes flew over bold black
script and she gave up a little prayer that her assumed name might not be found in its midst.

'The Rose and Crown,' June replied with an
odd little laugh, acknowledging her sister's extreme reaction to her news. 'Oh, I see! You fear that
his visit will be awkward for you, Sylvie.' June's
tone was reassuring, for she had found a reason for
her sister's consternation. 'Adam is perfectly so-
phisticated and would abhor, as would you, mention being made of his proposal.' When that
comfort failed to raise her sister's frowning countenance an inch from the parchment, she continued, 'You must admit it was good of him to seek
to protect your reputation. His chivalry to a sixteen-year-old might have been a little *de trop*, but

strange behaviour was understandable at such a distressing time…' June's voice tailed off into huskiness and a pained look pleated her brow.

Sylvie enclosed her sister in a firm embrace. She had no business to feel so sorry for herself. That *distressing* time—what an inadequate description of such horror!—had almost finished in dear June losing her life to a madman's revenge. Her sister had risked her own life to ensure that she made her escape from the evil maniac. 'Please, you must not think of it,' Sylvie begged. 'Now you have Jacob and there is no one deserves happiness more than you.' She reinforced her hug. 'And I am so grateful to you for saving me.'

June chuckled gruffly against her sister's pearly hair. 'I know. You have told me many times…so many that I would hear it no more, if you please. Shall we go shopping this afternoon?' She changed the subject with a brave smile. 'I should like to buy gloves and stockings from the draper's.'

Sylvie simply nodded while her eyes were again drawn to the Marquess's note. She devoured the few sentences that seemed to mock her anxiety and set her stomach to viperous writhing. She was not prepared and ready yet to see him! Her plan had been that she would be the one to first make contact, not have him thrust the moment upon her. Now she was put on the spot: before he arrived tomorrow at three o'clock to gladly accept the role of godfather to Jacob, she must somehow accost him in private and apprise him of all that had gone on.

She doubted he would deliberately be unkind, even if he still harboured grudges towards her for rudely rebuffing his proposal two years ago. He would not risk losing William's respect and friendship over something he obviously now deemed trivial. Her betrayal might simply come about because he was unaware of the necessity to be discreet. Why should he not make mention that he knew the Merediths' youngest daughter was now wed to John Vance? He was a notable visiting the area. He might perhaps be asked by any number of prominent townsfolk about his connections in Hertfordshire. Imagined conversations scattered sinister voices in her mind: *Silver Meredith? But surely she is now married to that chap John Vance.*

No…surely you are mistaken, my lord. I can't imagine what made you think so.

Sylvie glared in frustration at the note. Drat the man. Why could he not have stayed in London?

She forced her mind to investigate solutions and soon realised there were very few. She could set herself the task of composing a plausible yarn to explain why she had passed herself off as John's wife at the George and Dragon—a hysterical choke clogged her throat at that challenge to her powers of invention—or she could tell the truth and risk his disapproval and his disgust. Her chin tilted. What cared she for his opinion? He was hardly a model of propriety.

She had gleaned from overheard snippets over the years that Lord Malvern, or the Marquess of Rockingham as he now was, was no stranger to scandal. She comforted herself with Mrs Bragg's words: '*...He's no right to go a-sermonising to you young folk...*' Having discovered from that worthy that he was base enough not only to entertain his paramours at wayside inns but to share them with other men too, she considered the landlady's opinion sound. She doubted the Marquess of Rockingham would like it widely known that he had been canoodling with a demi-rep who styled herself Lady Townsend. Sylvie wondered how eminently suitable for the role of godfather June would deem him if she knew the depths to which he had sunk in his roistering. But for now she must keep that to herself. She managed a small smile as she handed June back her note. If he *did* think to betray her...well, she might just do the same to him.

* * *

'Rockingham!'

Adam turned his head to see a jovial-looking fellow entering his private dining room and bearing down on him. He flicked a hand in greeting, but the small sigh beneath his breath was audible. Within a second he had continued giving his late breakfast, and his newspaper, his full attention.

Guy Markham was not so easily put off. He strolled over, disengaged a chair from the table legs and sat down.

'Couldn't conceive it to be you, y'know,' he confided on a grin. 'Saw the crest on your coach from the Green Man so thought I'd come across and ask old Patchett if you were indeed about. Could've knocked me down with a feather when he said my lord Rockingham was lodging here. Wouldn't have thought the Rose and Crown was your style.'

Adam cut a thick slice of juicy beef and piled it on his plate. 'As you see, it is.'

Guy continued grinning at him. 'So what brings you into this neck of the woods? Country's no good at this time of year. Season's just started, ain't it?' Guy's attention slunk again to the joint and the aromatic loaf around which were scattered a variety of condiments.

Adam pushed a plate his way.

'Decent of you, Rockingham,' Guy remarked, immediately sawing himself a wedge of bread. It was soon joined on his plate by a hunk of rare beef. 'Why d'you come here?' Guy demanded.

'Are you visiting your parents?' Adam idly foiled the inquisitive interloper with a query of his own. He lifted the silver-topped decanter to replenish his cup.

'Wouldn't be here myself by choice,' Guy moaned, pulling the decanter close once his host had finished with it. 'Sister's finally snared herself a man, so we all got summoned to make plans. Pomeroy's the unlucky chap. Told him not to take those odds on that nag. Wouldn't listen. Now his pockets are severely to let and my mother's persuaded him there's only one way to fill 'em.'

Adam gave his friend a wry smile. 'I take it your sister approves of the strategy?'

Guy shrugged and frowned pensively into space. 'Hard to tell. She seemed right enough when I left her this morning. But then Janet's never happier than when the house is crammed with women with French accents bearing cloth and pins. Came out and left them all to it. Lace everywhere…' He shuddered and fortified his nerve with a swig of liquor.

After a short silence, in which Guy zealously applied himself to his free meal, he observed morosely, 'Not many of us left now.' He shook his head in disgust. 'Thought Pomeroy had more stamina.'

Adam raised an eyebrow at that.

'Went down too easy in my opinion. They all do. Couldn't believe it when Trelawney let me down. Said he never would, then he went and did it.'

Adam's quizzical expression became sardonic.

'Been leg-shackled, for years now. Said marriage wasn't for him. Not for me either, I said, then Ross went and did it. Damned inconvenient. I was lodging with him in Grosvenor Square at the time. Had to move out. Strange behaviour…' He shook his head, chewing and looking reflective.

'I hear he's blissfully happy with Elizabeth,' Adam mentioned, pushing away his plate and gaining his feet.

Seeing his host had had his fill, Guy dragged over the cloth the remnants of the repast and set about demolishing it before the servants cleared away the covers. With a full mouth he spluttered, 'So…*why* are you in the vicinity, Rockingham? Nothing much here to tempt you, y'know. Nothing much here to tempt *me*. In fact, I'm off tomorrow, whatever the women say.'

The Marquess of Rockingham was not attending; he had his arms over his head and was stretching out his athletic frame.

'Are *you* visiting?' Guy probed amiably.

Adam gave a vague nod.

'Mean of 'em not to put you up, ain't it?' Guy observed, hacking the final bloody morsels from the beef bone. 'Marquess shouldn't be expected to put up at the Rose and Crown.'

Adam seated himself again and drew away Guy's plate so he had his full attention. 'I'm visiting people, Markham, who had no notice of my arrival,' he informed with a lazy caution.

''Course…damned inconvenient for them, then,' Guy hastily amended before retrieving his plate with a single tentative finger. 'Who are they? Relations? Must know 'em myself if they're local. Tell you what, when you do your duty I'll come too, keep you company.'

'Very kind of you, Guy, but I'll endeavour to manage alone.' With that irony Adam pushed himself out of his chair and walked to the small casement. A large hand braced against black wormy timber and he glanced down. What he saw made his expression turn to stone.

Undeterred by his friend's rebuff, Guy scraped the meat left on his plate between some bread and strolled over to see what it was Rockingham had managed to find interesting.

After Guy had stared in the same direction for a few moments, a sly look slew to Adam's face. 'Tomboy, y'know, shoots a gun better than her own father. My sister says she's too wild for her own good. Could be jealous of her though.' He looked down at the top of a poke bonnet from which peeped pearly-blonde hair. 'For you can't deny she's a sweet looker.' His sandwich dropped away from his mouth and he craned his neck to peer out. ''Struth!' he exclaimed when Sylvie turned about to face the tavern again, and he saw what it was she was carrying. 'That's a baby, ain't it?'

Sylvie silently cursed Jacob's nursemaid as she paced back and forth, cuddling her nephew and keeping her hat brim out of his clutch. Molly could not have chosen to be insubordinate at a more inopportune moment.

They had arrived in the village a short while ago. On the journey from Windrush Jacob had become fractious with his teething. Molly had done her best to pacify him, but it seemed only Sylvie had the soothing touch. Thus Sylvie had offered to sit with the nursemaid and care for him while June went to choose her fripperies. Once her sister was safely occupied, Sylvie had hoped to leave Jacob cat-napping in Molly's care while she hunted down the Marquess. His coach, resplendent with gold crest, was visible in the courtyard of the inn, so she was reasonably confident of finding him within.

Molly, however, had outwitted her by making a speedier escape. As soon as her mistress was gone, the girl had complained of feeling queasy from the bumpy ride. Before Sylvie could arrest her, Molly had jumped down, saying she must get a cordial from the apothecary lest she be violently sick. The maidservant had certainly departed in that direction, but moments ago Sylvie had spotted her at a distance, slinking between cottages with a youth who resembled Frederick from Windrush's stables. With an instruction to the driver to wait, Sylvie had dismounted and set baby Jacob to mewling from the disturbance, as she had hurried off in the direction of the Rose and Crown.

Jacob hiccoughed and Sylvie patted at his back, simultaneously glancing about. It was market day and the stalls were set out on the green, situated near the Green Man. The few people left in the vicinity of the Rose and Crown were hurrying about their own business. She was relieved to note that nobody seemed interested in her.

It was hardly proper for a genteel young woman to enter such an establishment, let alone with her nephew grizzling in her arms. Sylvie sighed. Not much about her recent behaviour had been seemly, she had to admit.

'We seem destined to cross paths in tavern courtyards.'

Startled, Sylvie spun jerkily about. She quickly rubbed Jacob's back as he again screwed up his little face in readiness to howl. 'Heavens! You frightened me. Look, you have made the baby cry again.' The rebuke was delivered as she swayed her body to soothe Jacob.

'My apologies, Mrs Vance—'

'Don't call me that!' Sylvie hissed before he could properly conclude his apology.

Adam thrust his hands into his pockets. 'Why ever not?' His lids lowered thoughtfully—a simple question had made her blanch and sneak a furtive look about. His fear that she might dart immediately away was unfounded. In fact, she lingered, looking awkward. His dark gaze settled on the dewy-eyed infant bobbing in her arms. Her hip was jutting to accommodate his weight and a small slender hand was skilfully supporting a downy skull encased in a blue bonnet.

'Your son looks like you.'

Sylvie's jaw dropped and she glanced at Jacob before stuttering, 'You…you don't think that…?' Blood suffused her face. He believed her married; why would he not assume that a blond, blue-eyed child she was cuddling was her own? But there was no time for explanations. Quickly she drew a breath and gabbled, 'I must speak to you urgently and in private. But please do not question me now or address me as Mrs Vance.'

The low vibrancy in her words caused him to frown and tilt his head contemplatively. Intelligent dark eyes were fixed on her face with unwavering intent.

'I must tell you something before you visit my family tomorrow. It is a delicate matter.' She read from his face that, despite her plea not to, he was about to question her. She furiously shook her head. 'I am sorry! I can't say more until we are private!'

A shrug described his confusion, but he made no attempt to press her for further details.

'There is a derelict cottage on the track that leads to Windrush. It is about a half-mile past the turnpike and set back from the road. We must meet there.'

'This is very intriguing, Mrs…er…this is intriguing, madam,' Adam mimicked her whispering tone to correct himself. 'But I think you must tell me a little more…'

'Shh…just listen!' Sylvie snapped, for she was made indignant by that idle amusement in his eyes. 'There is not much time. June will soon be out of the draper's and looking for me… Oh, Heavens! There is Guy Markham. He *knows* me.'

'He knows me too. We've just had breakfast together.'

'You didn't mention me, did you?'

'Why would I?'

'Good,' Sylvie muttered, her anxiety preventing her retaliating to his strengthening mockery. 'Say nothing to him at all. You must meet me at the cottage this afternoon, at four o'clock. No…no; that is too soon. I shall not arrive by then: 'tis already past two.' She bit at her lip, frowning in consideration. 'Six o'clock is preferable and it will still be light.' In Sylvie's feverish mind a vital issue emerged. 'Do you know Bridge Cottage?'

'No, but the desire to discover what this is all about will surely help me find it.'

'Miss Meredith,' Guy boomed. 'How are you? Saw you from the window.' He tickled at little Jacob's ribs, making the peaceful child pucker his face in readiness to howl again.

'Bonny child.' Guy grimaced at the first screech and looked flustered.

Sylvie greeted him quickly before saying, 'I

must go…he—my nephew—is teething, you know.' With a final explicit stare at Adam, she turned and hurried back towards the coach.

'One of her sisters must be staying over at Windrush and given her the tot to mind.' Guy pulled a long face. 'Didn't mean to put her to the blush like that. Don't think she wanted to talk to me at all. Don't have much luck with women,' Guy volunteered dolefully.

Adam gave him a quizzical smile. A thought entered his mind and he tried to banish it. It stubbornly persisted, so he allowed himself to wonder whether *his* luck with the angelic chit might improve now she was married…

Chapter Six

'Am I very late?'

Sylvie's oblique greeting served as her apology too as Hazel plunged to a snorting stop by Bridge Cottage. She fondly massaged the mare's neck for, once they had managed to escape from the house, they had made good time to their rendezvous.

Having alighted from her little steed with boyish agility, she straightened her clothes, crumpled from the hectic dash over fields and fences. Sylvie realised it was as well her mother had not caught her riding astride in her stylishly tailored riding skirts; such gallivanting, even in breeches, offended her.

Had Mrs Meredith just observed her youngest daughter hoisting her hems to prevent them tripping her as she sprang to the turf—and in doing so giving the Marquess of Rockingham a most tantalising view of shapely calves and ankles—she would have attempted to box her youngest daughter's ears for the shame of it.

Despite pearly curls still jigging about her face, Sylvie felt quite composed as she brushed dust from her sleeves. She took a proper look at the elegant gentleman who was lounging against the grimy white-boarded exterior of Bridge Cottage. He was dressed in grey riding jacket of excellent quality and style. The chestnut hunter placidly cropping grass to his left looked equally impeccable. The Marquess looked every inch the powerful aristocrat and quite out of place beside such a hovel—and such a hoyden, Sylvie wryly acknowledged to herself as she abandoned an attempt to remove all the debris from her clothes or to fasten her windswept hat on her shimmering hair.

A stub of a cigar was flicked to the earth and ground beneath the toe of a polished boot. The scent of tobacco smoke eddied in the air. Adam raised his gaze from his foot to a face of fascinating beauty. He stared lazily at the young woman who had, with no effort at all, rushed blood to thicken his veins. His mistresses exercised an appetising sensuality to try and beguile him. This young madam accidentally allowed him a glimpse of leg and he felt as randy as a callow youth. Which brought him to thinking of John Vance. No doubt he felt a similar passion for his delectable young wife. He'd be a fool not to.

Aware she was coming under moody scrutiny, Sylvie felt her colour rising. He thought her conduct unbecoming. Her mother told her time and again it was, and that she ought to act with more decorum. She made a show of daintily tucking a spiral of blonde hair behind a small ear. With her chin high, she swept past him, inadvertently knocking her hip against his thigh. She skittered back from the physical contact and tethered Hazel to the branch closest. There were more important matters to focus on this afternoon, she impressed on herself, than his opinion of her ladylike qualities, or the butterflies that inhabited her stomach when he stared at her like that.

Adam noted her uneasiness and regretted letting his admiration become obvious. He fished in his pocket for his watch and gave it a cursory glance, although he already knew she was fifty minutes late. The timepiece disappeared back whence it came in a glint of gold. 'I must admit, I was beginning to think I might be at the wrong place. Either that or you intended having a joke at my expense.'

'I wish it were just that,' Sylvie muttered with

such earnestness that it caused a rueful smile to tug at his mouth. Quickly she explained the reason for her tardiness. 'Guy Markham's mother and his sister, Janet, came to visit late this afternoon and I could not get away. They are neighbours from down in the valley at Spire Park. Oh, of course you must know where they live as you are acquainted with Guy.' A wry grimace preceded, 'Janet has recently become engaged so they came to brag about their happy news.'

'Being saddled with Pomeroy's debts warrants celebration?' was Adam's dry rejoinder.

'You know Thomas Pomeroy?'

A brief nod answered her. 'He is one of my neighbours in Mayfair. But not for much longer, it seems. I've heard gossip that he's leased the house in Upper Brook Street to keep the shirt on his back. I hope for all concerned it doesn't end in a scandal.'

'Is it likely to?'

'Not if Pomeroy can wheedle an advance on the marriage settlement to beat off the most persistent of his creditors.'

Sylvie slanted him a look. Gossip, scandal— precisely the topics she wanted to discuss with him. Not because those things affected other families, because they might devastate hers. Nevertheless Pomeroy's misfortune seemed as good a link to her problems as was likely to present itself.

'My intention in bringing you here was to speak of a scandal, actually…or rather to attempt to avert one.' She watched for his reaction and was anxious when he showed her none. He was deliberately curbing his curiosity and thus forcing her to provoke it if she were to achieve what she had set out to do. As a silence lengthened between them she wished, oddly, he had subjected her to an immediate inquisition. There was a stubborn reticence within her that baulked at volunteering information.

She bit her lip and steadied her nerve. There was no need to be wary of him. Once he had been, as well as cordial, quite kind to her. Before she had rudely rebuffed his marriage proposal he had championed her in front of her papa and William. She could remember quite clearly the occasion he had denied thinking her silly for asking questions that her father deemed highly improper. Lord Malvern, as he had been then, had gently educated her in the ways of the world.

Now she must admit to having been embroiled in something that she knew was highly improper. Perhaps if she could restore a little of the rapport they had once shared…

She glanced about and her eye was drawn again

to the magnificent stallion. 'You have brought a fine mount with you to Hertfordshire.' A winsome smile curved her mouth as a slender hand found chestnut flanks. The animal bobbed its head in appreciation of the caress.

'He isn't mine. Guy loaned him to me.'

'Ah…' Sylvie murmured and continued stroking while she foraged in her mind for something else to say. Staying with the neutral subject of horses seemed appropriate, as did reminding him of his obligation to her. 'Did you recover your stallion from the thieves?'

He smiled ruefully. 'I did, but not through any bravery on my part, I have to confess. Mrs Bragg sent one of her stable lads to fetch help in tracking them down. Their encampment was quite close by. They were packing up to leave when the dragoons got there. I owe you a debt of gratitude.'

Sylvie smiled. 'I'm glad you got him back. I was angry when I saw what they were up to and couldn't let them get away with it.'

The sun was sinking low on the horizon, slanting gold at her eyes. She realised it was getting late. The atmosphere between them seemed quite mellow. He had acknowledged the favour she had done him; now perhaps he might like to reciprocate and do her a good turn. She kept Adam at the corner of her eye as she selected words. 'I expect you are wondering what catastrophe might have occurred for me to act so...dramatically earlier today.'

'Did you come out to the Rose and Crown specifically looking for me?'

Sylvie cocked her head to quite a haughty angle. Despite her hope that they might deal together harmoniously, she had immediately bridled at his arrogant tone. Eventually she said, 'Yes, I did.'

'I'm flattered,' he murmured.

'You've no need to be,' Sylvie countered sharply. 'I only sought you out because...'

'Because...?' he prompted.

Adam watched her small fingers fiddle again with the chestnut's reins. Her flawless features puckered as she sought an acceptable opening gambit. Oddly her confusion stirred in him unwanted sentiment. It prompted him to say what she was waiting to hear, albeit curtly. 'Why do you not want to be called Mrs Vance?'

His brusqueness brought a startled look to widen a pair of stormy blue eyes. Her tongue tip stroked away a tremor in her lower lip and the innocent teasing caused a low expletive to growl out of him. Sylvie heard his frustration and knew that he was growing impatient with her. Again she searched the jumble of nonsense in her mind for a few pertinent words.

Adam watched her inner struggle and tried to resist the tenderness that swept over him. She had had this effect on him once before. Then he had been infatuated with an enchanting maid. Now Sylvie Meredith was a woman, another man's wife; and she was searching for a way to tell him that he had witnessed her elopement.

He had spent the afternoon mulling over in his mind why she had seemed so desperate to divulge something quickly and privately. Two vital facts taken together produced one likely conclusion. A young couple travelling light along the Great North Road, displaying a distinct desire to be left alone, were usually runaways.

'You and Vance eloped, didn't you? I take it your parents are still distressed by it and you want to beg my tact and discretion when I visit tomorrow.'

Sylvie's gaze clung to his saturnine features while within relief and shock vied for precedence. 'Have you known all along?'

Adam lounged back against the peeling paint of the timbers and crossed his arms over his chest. 'No; but once you had hinted something was wrong it didn't take long to work out. After a lengthy gap in our acquaintance you must be annoyed that I've turned up twice recently at inopportune moments.' He paused; a hint of a smile touched his mouth at her eloquent silence. 'Why did you choose him?'

Sylvie's chin tilted. She had recognised the slightly disparaging reference to John and it irked. 'John Vance is a good friend of mine.'

'And that was enough to make you defy your parents, and convention, and elope with him?'

She nodded vigorously. 'I would much rather live with him than with a bullying lecher…' She noted his eyes immediately narrow and added quickly, 'Neither would I want a boring fop who passes for an eligible bachelor in polite society.'

'And to which group do I belong?' he asked quietly. 'Or perhaps you think I'd fit both.'

'You must have some conceit to think I included you at all.' A moment after that spontaneous proclamation she realised such truths were hardly likely to help her gain him as an ally. Besides, she had not at all been intending to insult him. 'I didn't mean…I was not referring to you. I'm sure you are not a bully or a bore.' The glaring omissions from her platitude made a cynical smile turn up a corner of his mouth.

His amusement needled her into qualifying her approval. 'I might have heard rumours about you, but I wouldn't pass judgement on your character without knowing you better.'

'I should quit now while you're being pleasantly complimentary,' he softly interrupted.

She did just that and bestowed on him such a grateful smile that it made him laugh.

'So let's talk of John Vance. You know Vance well and like him?'

'I have said so,' she answered rather stiltedly.

'I imagine your parents don't approve of him and want the fiasco kept quiet for as long as possible.' *Until they've groomed him into a worthy consort*, he was tempted to add, but he kept the notion to himself.

'My parents do like him, but naturally such an escapade has created…tension between our two families. None of it is John's fault,' she impressed on him. 'It was my idea. But if it gets out that we ran away together there will be a scandal.'

'The match is unequal, but hardly a scandal.'

Sylvie had for a while sensed a misconception was building between them. Her knowledge of what it was came simultaneously with Adam's enlightenment. Their eyes clashed and clung before Sylvie's skittered away. Sylvie was about to improve his knowledge when Adam snapped savagely, 'Which way along the Great North Road were you travelling that night?'

A mute defiance sprang up in her as his attitude changed from mild interest to anger.

'Which way?' Adam demanded to know.

'North!' she finally fired at him. 'We were travelling towards Scotland.'

'You were still unwed when you stayed overnight with him at the George and Dragon?'

Sylvie flushed, but managed to boldly hold his stare. She briefly nodded. 'There was but one chamber left, so we stayed there as man and wife.'

'So you did,' he drawled dulcetly. The knowledge that he could have taken Miss Sylvie Meredith home before she had a chance to journey on to Gretna Green ripped into Adam's mind. But for the chaos in the inn when his horse was stolen, he might have had a chance to question them both further about where they were bound.

It became clear now why they had slipped away so hastily when his back was turned for a moment the next morning. On reflection, he had excused that discourtesy as a mild awkwardness the couple might have felt at a chance meeting with a rejected suitor. But Vance was at that point her lover, not her husband. Little wonder Miss Meredith had looked embarrassed and eager to escape further questions. And little wonder she was desperate to keep details of the episode from general circulation. In fact, if he had dragged her home to her parents, he would have done them no favour whatsoever. Their youngest daughter, at that point, was already ruined. Still, he felt enraged that the opportunity to keep her single had been lost.

Vance had offered to help recover his stolen horse. The memory flooded his mind. If only he had insisted he do just that, he would have got the information he wanted. John Vance, he had deduced quite quickly after meeting him, would always be an easier nut to crack than this sharp-witted minx.

Now Sylvie Meredith was the wife of a man who, however inoffensive, wasn't good enough for her. He would hazard a tidy sum that her parents knew it and were feeling distraught for not having more closely guarded such a jewel.

As for the bride, he could tell from her defence of Vance that she also recognised it to be a *mésalliance*. 'If you're ashamed of your behaviour, or your husband, so be it, Mrs Vance. You need not fear that I will make mention of what I know to anyone at all. Good evening.' With that he snatched the chestnut's reins out of the tree.

He was going! His scorn was palpable, even if he

had so far managed to restrain himself from sneering or leering at her. How much stronger would be his disgust when he discovered the whole truth: that despite having spent the night with John, then setting out for Scotland, she was still a spinster.

She knew she ought feel ashamed, cowed perhaps for having so brazenly flouted sensibility, but she didn't. She felt incensed by his righteous attitude and by the fact that he deemed her capable of meanly despising John's status.

'How dare you turn your back on me as though I am not worth that!' A click of two slender fingers drew no response at all. 'How dare you think for one moment that I would marry a man, then refuse to acknowledge him as my husband because he was not good enough!' When he did not turn about Sylvie stormed up to him and grabbed his sleeve. 'John Vance is a friend. He is kind and loyal and…and…oh, he is everything that is nice!' A small booted foot ground into dust in frustration when he refused to respond and simply made ready to mount his horse. 'John might not be clever or eligible in the common way of things, but I would rather live my life with him than with a…a…vile philanderer who masquerades as a fine gentleman.'

Adam swung smoothly up into the saddle. 'Suddenly you have an opinion on my character, I see,' he said. 'It seems only fair that you should hear my opinion of you, Mrs Vance. The time that has elapsed since last we met has done nothing to improve you. You're still the infuriating brat you were at sixteen. You're also, by your own admission, not averse to acting like a shameless trollop. Your parents must be very proud of you.' He controlled the refreshed chestnut with a flick of the reins. 'As for your husband, he is welcome to you, my dear. Far from being not good enough for you, I fear Vance has got the worst of the deal. You may convey to him this vile philanderer's deepest condolences.'

Sylvie stared up at him, her face white with rage and humiliation. Her fists clenched against her skirts in a way that made him smile.

'Oh, whatever my feelings for you, I will not betray you. I have too much respect for William Pemberton for that. I have given you my word and will keep what I know to myself, but spare me the hypocrisy over your motives for asking for my silence. You married in haste and regret it no less than your parents. That's the truth—'

'No!'

Adam ignored her protestation. With a curt nod of his dark head, he allowed the horse its head and was soon galloping away from the cottage towards the road.

Sylvie felt a storm of emotion clogging her throat. Part of her wanted to find a stone to hurl at him in the hope of knocking him off his high and mighty perch. Part of her wanted to run after him, catch at his leg and drag him to a halt. She wanted to make him stay and listen. She wanted to conclude her tale, then be the first to leave. She wanted to chill him with contempt as he had just done to her.

Chapter Seven

'It's good to see you, sir.'

Adam met the outstretched hand and shook it, but disengaged his fingers when the fellow contested his grip. Perhaps the boy was trying to impress on him that he was now a man. 'You've grown since last we met,' Adam said to his godfather's son. 'I remember you were thin as a rake and about so high.' He held a hand out below his shoulder.

Hugo Robinson's fair complexion grew ruddy at a reminder of how slight had once been his stature. 'It must be more than nine years since you clapped eyes on me. I was only thirteen then.' It was a dismissive statement as he rammed burly fists in his pockets.

'Is it as long as that? It's odd that I recognised you straight away.' Adam looked over the lofty young man. Indeed, there was much about him that seemed familiar, and he knew a renewed acquaintance wasn't going to persuade him to like Hugo better than he had almost a decade ago.

As a child he had had a wild energy that could manifest itself in spitefulness. He had been apt to butt into adult conversations in a most precocious manner. But those were minor irritations. There was another reason why Adam's hackles stirred when in his company. Hugo had sly eyes, he realised. They might still be baby blue and make direct contact, but there was scant warmth or sincerity in their depths.

'I remember you spent a month with us at Rivendale.' A smile stretched Hugo's sanguine lips. 'It was good hunting that year. I bagged more birds than I could count.'

'I remember you did well,' Adam praised gently while wondering how two people as amiable and charming as Sir Anthony and Lady Robinson could have such unappealing progeny. It was a blessing, perhaps, that Hugo was an only child. Or perhaps his parents deemed it a curse.

'What brings you to the Rose and Crown so early?' Adam seated himself again at the breakfast table and gestured an invitation at his visitor to join him.

Hugo looked over the appetising food, but his eyes settled longest on the bottle of claret.

'I'm on an errand for my father. He would have come over himself, but he's not up to travelling far at the moment. His leg is swollen to hell.' Hugo told of his father's affliction with a chilling satisfaction. Adam's eyes narrowed on Hugo as he strolled to the door of the private dining room and looked out. 'Where's that Patchett when you need him?' Hugo muttered. 'I've a rare thirst for ale that needs attention.'

'You look as though you attended to your thirst last night.'

'That's why I've a need for ale.' Hugo guffawed. 'I think brandy turns my tongue to wool. It needs a washing.' He grimaced distaste with his mouth, then looked again at the bottle. 'Would you mind…?'

An easy shrug gave him permission to help himself and he immediately did so.

Adam had already noted the early signs of dissipation carved into the youthful features of Hugo Robinson. His eyes were lightly bloodshot and, despite his constant grins this morning, his fleshy mouth had a cynical droop. But he was a handsome man. He was of good height and breadth and his hair was butter blond. Those attributes, coupled with his status as heir to a baronetcy and a fine estate, probably rendered him attractive to the ladies hereabouts. He watched as Hugo forked five fingers across his scalp, then dispatched his wine in two gulps.

'My father's directed me to bring you back to Rivendale,' Hugo announced, depositing his empty cup. 'He was quite put out when you sent word you were staying at the Rose and Crown. He bids me say you must stay with us and won't hear otherwise. Here…my mother's written a note insisting you arrive in time for dinner.'

Adam took the letter and broke the seal. He scanned the invitation and pocketed it with a small smile. Lady Robinson's sweetness shone through in her prose.

'Thank them for the offer of hospitality, but I'm only in Hertfordshire till tomorrow, then am back to London. I would not put your parents to the trouble of getting a room ready to accommodate me. I'm comfortable enough here for a short stay. But I look forward to seeing them, and gladly accept the invitation to dine at seven.'

Hugo again helped himself to the decanter just as a serving maid tapped at the door and entered the room. As she saw the Marquess had company, her shy smile shrivelled and she looked ready to shrink back through the aperture.

'I'm finished,' Adam told her and beckoned her in to clear the breakfast covers.

The girl seemed unwilling to obey. Finally she forced herself jerkily forward and, skirting the furniture, came to the table. Only once did she raise her eyes from the floor and that was to shoot a measuring glance at Hugo, as though to gauge his position.

Adam studied her behaviour with a frown on his face. She was a pretty maid, perhaps fourteen, and well endowed with female charms for one so young. She had not previously shown herself to be self-conscious or nervous in his presence.

A glance at Hugo was enlightening. He was eyeing her with lascivious interest. It was obvious the girl was not flattered by his attention; in fact, she looked terrified. Adam glanced thoughtfully at Hugo; perhaps he had misjudged this man's popularity with the local girls. If anything, he would hazard a guess he had a predatory reputation.

'I don't say I blame you for choosing to bed down at the Rose and Crown, my lord. There are sweet advantages,' Hugo insinuated with enough volume for the girl to hear him as she slipped from the room carrying silverware. 'The Patchett wenches are all obliging.' He glanced slyly at the Marquess, a wolfish smile just baring his teeth.

'She's just a child; hardly of interest to me,' Adam said coldly. He pushed himself back from the table and stood up.

His disgust was not solely prompted by Hugo's lechery. What right had he to act the moralist? He had been older by several years than was this man when he had paid attention to a sixteen-year-old. It was true his intentions on that occasion had been honourable. Nevertheless, he ought to have known that Silver Meredith had been far too young—not only in years—to deal with a man such as he. Or perhaps he had known, but was too selfish to let her immaturity deter him. He'd wanted her and only cowardice and hypocrisy had previously stood in the way of him acknowledging it. Suddenly he wanted to be left alone.

'If you'll excuse me, Hugo, I've several calls to make today while I'm in the vicinity and I don't want to arrive late to dine at Rivendale.'

Hugo looked disinclined to take the hint to leave. 'You know other families in the area?'

'Yes,' Adam said while pointedly consulting his watch.

Hugo bridled at that unsubtle dismissal; nevertheless he forced an insouciant grin as he sauntered to the door. 'I imagine the Markhams are on your list. They're the most important landowners around here...after us.'

'Guy Markham is an acquaintance,' Adam confirmed.

Hugo turned in the doorway as though a thought had just occurred to him. 'Do you know the Merediths?'

'William Pemberton married into the Meredith family. He's a very good friend of mine.'

'If you are to visit the Merediths, you might see my future wife.' It was an announcement designed to recapture the Marquess's attention. It succeeded immediately, but not for any reason that Hugo could possibly have guessed.

'Future wife?' Adam echoed softly, strolling closer.

'Silver Meredith is her name. Her family call her Sylvie. I expect you've heard of her as Pemberton is married to her sister.' When that oblique question remained unanswered, Hugo continued, 'It's all arranged, but not yet official. Our mothers have been friends for years. Just a few minor details need to be agreed, then our betrothal will be announced. It's a good match for her. She'll be Lady Robinson one day, when I inherit my birthright.' With a lewd smile he added, 'I'll concede I'm lucky too. I can hardly wait for sweet Sylvie to be all mine.'

Aware that he'd completely captured Adam's interest, he hooted gleefully. 'I've surprised you,

I can see. Perhaps you think I am too young to get myself leg-shackled. But wait till you see her. She's a beauty, if too headstrong for what's considered nice in a wife. But that will change when we're married.' He executed a small bow and went out, whistling and looking vastly pleased with himself.

'You are not going to vex me and say you are going out when the Marquess is due shortly?'

'No.' A single word from Sylvie answered her mother's tart enquiry.

'Oh… Oh, good. That is good. 'T'would be rude of you to avoid seeing him.' Gloria relinquished her grip on the doorknob and came further into her daughter's bedroom.

'I shan't avoid him,' Sylvie reassured her and continued with an attempt to combat the tangles in her unruly tresses. She had taken her morning ride as usual even though the wind had been strong enough to whip the hat from her head and the pins from her chignon.

Gloria stood by her daughter's dressing stool and watched a gleam being brushed into hair the colour of moonlight. For a moment Gloria proudly studied an oval visage blessed with perfect features. All four of her daughters were attractive, and she had been pleased to accept compliments on their good looks, but her little Sylvie was sculpted like a goddess in face and figure. Her cheekbones were high and honed, her lips perfectly bowed and she was taller and more willowy than the others. 'You know, Sylvie, if you had accepted Adam Townsend when he did you the honour of asking you to marry him, all this…' a whirling hand described the chaos of her aborted elopement '…would not have occurred. You would have made a most beautiful couple. You would now be a happily married woman.'

'I doubt that I would be anything more than married, Mama. And I think you know it too.' Sylvie continued serenely stroking the brush through her hair. 'The Earl of Malvern—' she tutted away the mistake '—the Marquess of Rockingham, I should say, has the reputation of a degenerate.'

Gloria cleared her throat. 'Rockinghams have always been rather notorious in that way—debauchery and so on. Rumour and speculation…I'm sure that is all it is.'

Sylvie gave her mother a wry smile, wondering what her reaction would be should she inform her that the new Marquess had entertained a doxy at a wayside inn. And that was no rumour, for she had seen the wanton with her own eyes.

What needled her until her insides squirmed was that yesterday she had not had the opportunity to flail him with her knowledge. He had managed to batter her pride with a stinging reprimand, then had fled the scene before she had time to reciprocate.

But there was yet time. Oh, she was going nowhere this afternoon when their august guest graced them with his presence. All that disturbed her was how they might find an opportunity to be private. There was unfinished business between them and she would ensure that this time he stayed within earshot until she had told him exactly what she thought of him. Hypocrite, he had called her. *Her!* She'd give him hypocrite!

Gloria closely observed her daughter's mobile expression as she grappled with her inner thoughts. It seemed mention of Adam Townsend produced in her daughter quite vehement emotions. She fiddled nervously with her lace handkerchief as her daughter again agitatedly chewed at her soft lips. 'You will mind your manners with the Marquess, Sylvie, won't you?'

Sylvie glanced up innocently on recognising her mother's suspicions.

'He is a most influential gentleman and of course your brother-in-law's good friend. The

Marquess is to be little Jacob's godfather. It wouldn't do if you should…upset him.'

Sylvie bent her head. She spoke through a tumble of silver silk as she recommenced burnishing her hair. 'Don't fret so, Mama. I promise I shall treat the Marquess with no less respect than he shows me.'

Gloria felt her spirits soar. She would be the happiest woman alive if the Marquess were to renew his interest in her youngest daughter. She again sent a glance sliding between the couple and felt an excited tremor pass through her. She was right! They were exchanging most meaningful looks.

Heaven knew he was handsome enough to make a nun abscond from a convent. Plus he was so charmingly nonchalant. He had taken Jacob on to his lap and not turned one immaculate hair when the boy had regurgitated some milk on his coat. He had simply cleaned it off with a handkerchief. She had noticed that Sylvie seemed amused at the mishap, but then it was a good sign that not even the recent disaster could dampen her sense of humour. William, who was nobody's fool, held Adam Townsend in high esteem, and little wonder, for the Marquess was perfectly pleasant in every way.

She turned her attention to her model child.

Sylvie was being unstintingly helpful, assisting with distributing tea and keeping little Jacob happy by bringing him his toys. She certainly was on her best behaviour. And Gloria felt sure there was only one person her daughter sought to impress.

'I shall ring for Molly. I think it is time for Jacob's nap,' June said, casting a maternal eye on her son. He was bobbing about on the rug and screwing his little face in readiness to cry.

'I'll take him upstairs,' Sylvie offered, and gathered the child into her arms. For some time she had been keen to escape the stifling atmosphere in the small drawing room. She was sure that their illustrious visitor was equally aware of the tension strung between them like wire. His air of vague amusement probably sprang from an assumption that she was itching to continue their argument. He must also have noticed her mother's unsubtle fawning.

Her mother had been giving her little smiles and nods for more than an hour, sanctioning her polite conduct with the Marquess. Only he knew just how much she had yearned to throw his tea into his lap rather than place it daintily by his side.

But he had kept to his word. There had been no hint that he knew about her recent elopement. He thought she was Mrs John Vance, yet so far he had avoided addressing her by any name at all.

'Might I be allowed to see my godson's nursery at Windrush?' It was an odd request, tantamount to a gentleman showing interest in investigating the kitchens. But Sylvie knew why it had been made. He was acquiescing to her latent demand that they talk privately.

Edgar and William were standing close to a table with their heads bowed. Now Edgar jerked his eyes away from a compulsive contemplation of ivory pieces that had been stationed since yesterday on a chessboard. The game with William had gone on long into the night and was evenly scored so far. It was their intention to resume the battle after dinner. William glanced about, surprise barely perceptible in his voice as he immediately offered to indulge his friend's eccentricity. 'I'll show you, if you like…'

'Sylvie will do it,' Gloria interjected quickly with a bright smile for her son-in-law. 'There is no need for you to disturb yourself, William. Sylvie has offered to take Jacob to his bed.'

The room was rather quiet as Adam held the door open for Sylvie, burdened with her whimpering nephew. Before they were fully in the corridor Gloria began voicing jolly opinions on the fine weather.

Once they were on the first-floor landing, having gained that elevation without a word passing between them, Sylvie hissed, 'Wait here. I hardly think that Jacob's nursery is a fit place for an argument.'

'Are we to argue, then?'

'Oh, yes.'

Adam's dark eyes flowed over the mutinous profile presented to him. 'Are you about to punish me for not allowing you the last word yesterday, Mrs Vance?'

Sylvie tilted her head and narrowed her eyes at him. She would not give him the satisfaction of hearing her say he was right…even though he was. But sense dictated that she must temper her resentment and conclude her confession. She must yet disabuse him of a belief that she had married following her elopement, for that misconception, if innocently let slip, might cause serious problems for the Merediths.

'Where is the bridegroom? Is he banished to the stables when you have company?'

'I am not ashamed of John! And I wish you would not constantly insinuate that I am!' The words were quietly sibilant to protect the tenuous slumber of the child in her arms. Then with a toss of her head she walked on, barely allowing herself to glance back to see whether he had obeyed and was waiting for her to return.

* * *

'You're out of breath,' Adam noted lightly as Sylvie sped up to him, having settled Jacob. 'Were you rushing back to see me?'

'To see if you had slunk away while my back was turned!' Sylvie snapped. 'You managed to flee yesterday once you had bullied me into listening to all you had to say.'

'*Me* bully *you*?' Adam laughed. 'So far, my dear, I think our entire acquaintance has been founded on you mistreating me. I seem to recall getting my shins kicked and my face slapped two years ago when all I had in mind was protecting you. More recently you nagged me into meeting you at Bridge Cottage. You just ordered me to wait here for you. When you aren't employing that acid tongue of yours, you're flaying me with those devastating eyes. If looks could kill, I would have expired long since. Does your husband know he married a shrew?'

That took the gale out of Sylvie's sails and she blushed in shock and embarrassment. 'I would never seek to intimidate anyone!' she insisted, outraged. 'I hate bullies. I was hysterical with fear for June's safety when I kicked you… Oh, you know all this and are simply saying it to vex me. How could I possibly dominate you? I imagine never in your life have you been bullied, or done anything you didn't want to.'

Adam managed to conceal a grin at her defensiveness. 'Don't fret over it. I confess there might be a desirable element in the thought of being dominated by you…'

A wary look was peeped at him from beneath her lashes. Their odd discourse had put that fierce warmth back in his eyes. He seemed closer to her than before, and she felt a little stifled by his overpowering body. 'We can't talk privately here.' She quickly hopped down a step away from him. 'I shall show you the grounds. Papa has designed a new pond that is in a secluded part of the walled garden. It is just finished and has some rather fine fish in it…from the East.'

Adam strolled about the rectangle of water, his head bowed and his hands in his pockets.

'There's one…look!' Sylvie pointed quite excitedly as a flash of gold broke the surface of the water. She raised proud eyes as a small shimmering shoal gathered beneath the rainbow droplets of the fountain. Adam was looking in the general direction she had indicated, but his expression was still stubbornly dispassionate.

A sense of uneasiness stole over Sylvie. She felt

less confident about haranguing him than she had whilst indoors. He seemed to have withdrawn from her into preoccupation. Yesterday he had called her an infuriating brat; today he had said she acted like a bully and a shrew. Still she hesitated in reciprocating with some choice epithets levelled at him. She sensed that he knew more of her business than she had disclosed, and that he was brooding on his knowledge.

Perhaps he had guessed—or prised from William—that she had never completed that journey to Scotland. Perhaps he was waiting for her to admit she was ruined. But then earlier he had referred to her as Mrs Vance, and to John as her bridegroom, without a hint of sarcasm. She sighed. The only way to find out what he knew was to ask.

'I think you have a further opinion on my behaviour,' she suggested carefully. She was standing directly opposite him and their eyes merged through a jet of crystal droplets.

'I have. But Heaven forbid that I should voice it before you have a chance to deliver your speech. I don't want you accusing me again of riding roughshod over you.'

Suddenly Sylvie wanted very much to hear what it was he knew. She wanted to weigh the information in her mind and deduce if it might be a help or hindrance. 'No, please. You are a guest. Guests must go first.' It was earnestly said and the sweet smile that ensued caused him to silently laugh. He was not fooled by her faux charm, but tenaciously she clung to her demure attitude and gestured daintily for him to speak.

Adam strolled about the pond, holding her eyes with his until he was standing quite close. He looked down into a face of such pure beauty that he sensed his breath catch in his throat. He felt suddenly relieved that she had married John Vance before Hugo Robinson could get to her.

'Are you intending to tell your fiancé that you've eloped with another man?'

Chapter Eight

'*Fiancé?*'

Adam had to allow that her bewilderment seemed genuine. Either she did not know what on earth he was talking about or she was a fine actress.

'Hugo Robinson came to the Rose and Crown this morning to deliver me an invitation to dine at Rivendale. During the course of our conversation he informed me that there was a long-standing arrangement between you. He said you were unofficially betrothed to him.'

'That's a lie!'

'Is it? It is certainly no longer possible, in view of the fact you are married to someone else.'

'You didn't *tell* him that?' Sylvie choked out in a whisper.

Adam shook his head. 'When he finds out—as

he surely will—he will not be best pleased. He seems eager to have you as his wife.'

That information made the colour flee Sylvie's cheeks, depleting their golden glow. It was the very thought of such an awful future that had prompted her to abscond with John. 'Well, he must bear the disappointment, for I shall never marry him!' A horrible thought suddenly set her stomach squirming. She turned an indignant glare on Adam. 'Have you been *discussing* me with that oaf?' The accusation was damning and earned her a stern look.

'I didn't refer to you once,' Adam informed coolly. 'Not least because it would prove difficult knowing which name to choose.'

Sylvie had the grace to blush a little at that pointed reminder of her predicament. 'Thank you for that,' she mumbled, slanting a meek peek at him. 'I dislike Hugo and he knows it. There has never been a proper arrangement between us.'

'*Proper?*' He selected the word that interested him, echoing it back at her in a tone of dark irony.

Sylvie attempted to quash his curiosity with eyes that sparked violet fire. When he simply plunged his hands into his pockets in a show of tedium, she explained tersely, 'Our parents are friends and hoped we might form an attachment. My mother, especially, favours the match…but then she does not know Hugo's true character. Sir Anthony and Lady Robinson are nice people, but I go rarely to Rivendale simply so I might avoid their son.'

'You said yesterday you would rather be married to Vance than a lecherous bully. Were you referring to Hugo?'

Spontaneously Sylvie nodded, then quickly frowned and shook her head. A hand pressed to her forehead in frustration.

By allowing him to know of her aversion to Hugo, she had foolishly again whetted his curiosity. But she was loath to disclose any more. The Marquess was obviously well acquainted with the Robinsons, perhaps related to them in some way. He had so far respected her wishes and said nothing about her elopement, but if his loyalties were divided…what then? And what would he think if he knew what prompted her hatred of Hugo? Would he declare—as Hugo had—that her behaviour had been wanton enough to excite a man's base passion?

Hugo was in private a brute, yet when socialising in polite circles he strove to maintain a façade of charming respectability. The way he sucked up to her mother and her friends made Sylvie feel bilious.

Adam had said he was to dine at Rivendale this evening. Her name might again crop up in conversation. For how much longer could she expect him to defend her? She could not blame him for tiring of this game of secrets. The Marquess of Rockingham might be a libertine, but she was sure he was also honest and forthright, and very adult. He was in every way as far removed from Hugo as a man could be.

Huge solemn eyes raised, scanned hard masculine features for a sign he might still be lenient and willing to protect her. 'How do you know the Robinsons? I have not heard Lady Robinson mention your name.'

'I have been remiss in keeping in touch with them. It is almost a decade since I visited my godfather at home, although I often meet up with Sir Anthony in town.'

'He is your godfather.' Sylvie murmured the information to herself.

'What was it you wanted to say to me?' For a while Adam had sensed that her pique, simmering since their confrontation yesterday, was withering. Not because she had warmed towards him, but because something graver was now troubling her. He too had been preoccupied, pondering an odd phrase that had lodged in his mind. *'My mother es-*

pecially favours the match...' she had said moments ago.

Unless the woman was promoting bigamy, it was surely nonsense to talk of it in the present tense, unless... An explosive thought made him suddenly curse himself for a fool. He had too readily concluded that the lovers had reached their destination, thus overlooking a glaringly obvious possibility: they might have been apprehended before they reached Gretna Green.

On arrival at Windrush he had been a trifle surprised to see Mr and Mrs Meredith in such good spirits. Their exquisitely lovely daughter might have married beneath her, and mention of her elopement might be taboo, but nevertheless they entertained with aplomb. When Gloria Meredith assisted him in being alone with Sylvie his thoughts had turned cynical. It was not unknown for an influential friend to be sought for a well-bred young woman deemed to have lowered her status by marrying a lesser mortal. If he was truthful, it had also already occurred to him that he could approach Sylvie once a decent period had elapsed since her elopement. The ambition remained unvanquished by his conscience.

But perhaps Gloria Meredith was not seeking to reinstate her daughter illicitly. If his suspicions were founded, the Merediths would be understandably desperate to get Sylvie married before it leaked out that she was ruined.

Adam studied a profile of classically perfect proportions that was inclined towards the water. Flashes of silver and gold were intermittently visible beneath the surface. 'Tell me the truth: are you married to Vance?'

Her head jerked up and the mix of relief and shame shining from Sylvie's eyes spoke for her.

'You have deliberately encouraged me to think you're his wife.'

The icy tone in which that was delivered stirred Sylvie's hackles. 'I have not! Well…I might have done, at first, but there was no choice. How was I to know that you would turn up at such a bad time? We had to present ourselves as Mr and Mrs Vance at the inn, for propriety's sake. But it was a pointless lie, for Mrs Bragg guessed the truth.'

'Obviously Mrs Bragg is more astute than I am,' Adam said with a self-deprecatory laugh.

Sylvie gave him a wry smile. 'I fear she makes sure she knows all her guests' business.'

'Are you hinting that she knew mine?'

As the silence lengthened it became obvious he expected her to explain what was meant by her subtle smile.

Sylvie remained uncommunicative; she wasn't prepared to risk provoking him by repeating Mrs Bragg's theory on the nature of his companion that night. Abruptly she sank down in a billow of blue muslin to crouch by the side of the pond. She stirred the water with a finger until several fish gathered close by. 'They expect me to feed them. I shouldn't really torment them… I wanted to tell you the truth; *tried* to tell you when we met at the cottage,' she suddenly burst out. 'But you stormed off before I had a chance to make my confession. I was about to own up today, but as you have guessed it all, I don't need to,' she finished lamely. Her eyes skittered away from features seemingly hewn from stone. 'You do see, don't you, why you must promise not to mention meeting us at the George and Dragon and so on?'

Adam suppressed a harsh laugh. 'Indeed I do see, Miss Meredith. I see a lot of things. Not least why your mother seemed keen just now to bring us together. You haven't told your family that I saw you at the George and Dragon, have you?'

'Heavens, no! They would be so ashamed. It's no exaggeration to say my mother might swoon dead away. You must say nothing to them. Promise me that you will not!' she ordered in agitation as she sprang up from the pond and shook dry her finger.

'I'm not sure I can do any such thing,' Adam said evenly. 'Your mother might take it into her head to try and manoeuvre me into again compromising you. Perhaps she hopes I will once again feel obliged to act the chivalrous fool and renew my proposal.'

His sarcasm made Sylvie's rosy lips form a bud, but guilty colour seeped into her face—his assessment of her mother's aspirations was probably sound. Nevertheless she retaliated with, 'I don't believe you would ever allow yourself to be cornered by anyone.'

'Your faith in my sturdy nature is touching, Miss Meredith. Are you reconsidering your opinion of me?'

Sylvie sent him a quelling look.

'If you can't stomach marrying Hugo Robinson, I would suggest your father takes a shotgun over to the Vances' farm and threatens to use it. Early wedding nights can produce unwanted consequences. Marry your lover with all due haste.'

With a perfunctory bow he strode past her, heading for the gate that opened a path through crumbling stocks en route to the house.

After a moment Sylvie conquered her shock and humiliation at being abruptly dismissed and flew after him. She grabbed at his arm, tugging at it until he spun about and came after her so quickly she was forced into a stumbling retreat.

'You are trying my patience, Miss Meredith.'

'And you as usual are greatly annoying me!' was shouted back at him. 'I'm not bothered by your insults. Let me tell you that John would deem it a privilege to marry me this very day and without a single shotgun in evidence.'

'I'm relieved to hear it,' Adam drawled before again pivoting on his heel.

Sylvie yanked on his sleeve, her face livid.

'What is it you want?' he bit out.

'Not you, that is for sure!' Sylvie cried. 'You are the most…the most aggravating man I have ever met!'

'Apart from Vance, is there a man you do like?' he enquired sarcastically. 'Hugo Robinson is an oaf; I'm aggravating and, as I recall, you have other complaints about my character.'

'And there is more I could mention—*will* mention,' Sylvie shrilled while her hands balled into fists at her sides. 'But first let me make one thing clear. I do not expect or want you to renew your proposal. I would not marry you should you go down on not one but both knees and beg me humbly to do so.'

'I promise you will never be subjected to any

such ludicrous sight, ma'am,' he avowed. As he loosened the gate latch an amused chuckle drifted back to her, making her insides writhe.

'Don't you dare laugh at me, or go before I have finished speaking,' Sylvie warned him, stamping a dainty shoe on to granite. 'I will not have it again. You ran away yesterday, you coward, before I had a chance to say my piece.'

Adam turned about and leaned back on rusty wrought iron, his arms crossed over his chest. 'You might have lost your innocence…' deep brown eyes flowed insolently over her body in a way that made Sylvie's face flame '…but it's not helped to improve you. You're still a tiresome child.' He strolled towards her, cocked his head to study her furious face. 'Perhaps you ought encourage Hugo; he might be more skilled than Vance at making a girl a woman.'

Sylvie visibly flinched as though he had struck her and tears glossed her vision.

Adam closed his eyes in shame and frustration. He could see that he'd wounded her deeply by patronising her swain and he regretted what he'd said. Yet he still felt inexplicably angry. And it was not simply because she had become embroiled in the sort of escapade that polite society would relish unearthing. Silver Meredith and her family would be the butt of ridicule for years to come if the scandal leaked out.

In a controlled tone he said quietly, 'Say what you must and have done quickly. I have a dinner appointment to keep.'

Sylvie feigned unconcern at his cold disgust. A swift movement dashed away her tears. 'I don't care how pressed for time you are, my lord. You will stay this time until you have heard me out. Let me start by saying that it was always my intention to confess to you that I had lied about being Mrs John Vance. I hoped, because once we were acquainted, that you would be tolerant when you heard the circumstances. And, in case you later accuse me of not being completely honest with you, I shall correct a misconception you have. We were not apprehended on the Great North Road, but turned back of our own volition.' Sylvie put up her chin and unswervingly met his dark eyes. 'That apart, I think that you have the nerve of the devil to have accused *me* yesterday of being a hypocrite. What right have you to act so pious? I doubt you would want to broadcast your reason for being at the George and Dragon. You might have witnessed *my* sin, but then *I* witnessed *yours* too.' With that Sylvie snatched her pastel skirts in vibrating fists and attempted to sweep past him.

'Indeed?' he said, his expression quizzical as he easily blocked her escape route with his powerful body. 'It's true I don't want my purpose in being there widely known. But enlighten me as to what you suspect were my misdeeds perpetrated beneath Mrs Bragg's roof.'

His expression was veiled, but she knew she had provoked his ire. She sensed a terrified exhilaration tremble through her. 'You don't seem quite so eager to leave now, my lord,' she taunted. 'Let me put your mind at rest. I will not disclose what I know. But if you are horrible to me, and betray me from spite, I will do the same to you.'

From between a web of black lashes a burning look seared her face. 'You think I would do that? Betray you from spite? Why? Because once I was foolish enough to propose to a silly little girl who could not even decline becoming a countess with a semblance of good manners? Do you think that matters to me now? It barely mattered to me then. When I asked you to marry me I was being chivalrous, nothing more.'

'You wanted to marry me, I know you did,' Sylvie insisted, staring up into eyes that now looked black as jet. 'I might have been young and quite naïve, but I could tell that you wanted to kiss me.'

Adam looked at soft lips slanted mutinously

and felt every shred of self-control slip away. 'Did you?' he purred. 'Well, this shouldn't come as a surprise, then.'

He gripped the tops of her arms and lifted her close so swiftly that her head swayed back, exposing a tantalising column of silken throat. His hungry mouth closed on warm flesh, tasting her skin before covering her lips.

'Get off! Don't!' Sylvie gasped against his face and then trembled into stillness.

John had pressed his lips to hers once or twice, and although it had not been unpleasant, she had dismissed kissing as rather boring. Her honest opinion had seemed to deter John from doing so again. Then Hugo Robinson had lured her to meet him that awful time. He had assaulted her mouth with his slimy tongue and teeth until she had retched. And then he had done more that was repulsive and she had vowed no man would ever be allowed to get away with it again.

But this wasn't disgusting. Adam was kissing her and making a new and magical sensation weaken her limbs. Her fists, hard against his chest, were relaxing, her lips softly parting. She felt the tip of his tongue touch hers and recoiled. When his fingers curved over her scalp to keep her close she fought in earnest.

Adam released her and she stumbled back with fingers pressed to her pulsing mouth. 'Don't ever do that again or…'

'Or…?' Adam echoed, while watching her closely. When she refused to elaborate he asked quietly, 'Why not?'

'Just don't do it,' Sylvie warned and turned away. He would not make her run from him. She would never run from a man again. She had fled from Hugo, with his blood beneath her fingernails and the sound of his coarse oaths in her ears. Her ripped and gaping clothes had flapped about her palsied limbs as she ducked and dodged branches and briars and pelted to safety.

With unsteady fingers she opened the gate and passed through it.

'Aren't you forgetting something?'

Sylvie turned about and put her head to a haughty angle.

'You haven't yet told me how I sinned at the George and Dragon. Come, tell me what it is you think you know about me.'

'I know that the woman you were with is not your wife. June says you have never been married. I would say *Lady Townsend* is a harlot. Mrs Bragg was of the same opinion and said that another gentleman was in her chamber too.'

She stepped back towards him and challenged him with flashing stormy eyes. 'Well? Are you about to deny any of it?'

'No. You are right in every respect. Lady Townsend is a harlot, I am afraid,' he replied with studied gravity. 'Unfortunately, she is also my sister-in-law so is able to use the title bestowed on her when she married my brother.'

Sylvie blinked as she digested that astonishing information.

'It seems you and Theresa had much in common that day. She was also ensconced with her lover and had no more success than you in masquerading before Mrs Bragg as a respectable lady.'

Sylvie felt her face flush at that insult. 'Are you about to tell me you were there on a mission of mercy?' she scoffed. 'Can your brother not fetch home his own wife?'

'Unfortunately not.' Adam was silent for a moment and his face tightened to a mask. 'He was crippled in the war and is virtually house-bound.'

Sylvie's eyes widened before her lashes fluttered low. Huskily she said, 'I'm sorry…'

Adam tilted a mirthless smile. 'Yes, I'm sorry too,' he said quietly and walked past her and back towards the house.

Chapter Nine

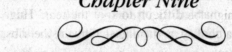

'I see she's finally got a ring on her finger.'

Guy Markham bristled on hearing that sneering comment on his sister's betrothal. 'No need to say it like that, you know. Janet is just twenty-three and a fine catch.' Guy worked his cravat away from his hot neck while whipping a glare at Hugo Robinson. He might be a guest at Rivendale, and this rude puppy might be the son of a baronet, but he was not too timid to demand the fellow step outside with him.

Hugo remained unmoved by the reprimand. He loosed an insolent gaze at a tall, stocky young lady with mouse-brown hair. She was inspecting the buffet whilst chattering to a woman who looked to be a faded version of her. 'I'm sure your mother is looking forward to having a son-in-law at last, even if it is Pomeroy. When is the wedding?' he asked idly.

'June. Fine time, so I am told by the ladies. Flowers, food, dresses…all at their best and so on,' Guy knowledgeably imparted. 'Having a marquee put up in the grounds at Spire Park.'

'Is that wise? If your sister's decked out in white silk, it might be difficult to spot the tent.' Hugo snorted a guffaw and nudged Guy in the ribs. 'Pomeroy's going to have his hands full that night…'

Guy slammed down his drink. 'See here, Robinson,' he gritted out, 'that's the outside of enough. Any more of your vile innuendo and I'll call for seconds.' Guy's face was ruddy with fury and his fists were balled at his sides.

Hugo patronisingly patted his shoulder. 'Calm down, man. God's teeth! Just being jocular, that's all…' The words were soothing, yet malicious satisfaction fired his eyes at having riled Guy. 'Speaking of marquees, where is our illustrious visitor to Hertfordshire? I was sure Rockingham was expected this evening. I know my parents issued him an invitation when he visited us earlier in the week.'

Guy ignored him for a moment. He was still smarting from having endured listening to his sister being ridiculed. 'I haven't seen him for a day or two.' The information was barked out. 'I recall he said he could not stay long in Hertfordshire. He has family business to attend to.' Guy excused himself in a mutter and turned on his heel.

Hugo gripped at his arm and nodded in the direction of the double doors. 'Now here's a certain young lady who certainly does take my fancy.'

Guy glanced in the same direction to see the Meredith family being greeted by the host and hostess. The sight of the new arrivals was welcome. Had pleasant company not soon appeared he would have upset his mother and sister, not to mention Sir Anthony and Lady Robinson, by taking off regrettably early simply to distance himself from this boor.

Before today, Guy had not held a strong opinion on Hugo Robinson. There was a decade or more between their ages and, although they had both been reared in the vicinity, they rarely socialised in the same circles. Now Guy felt glad to have finally had an opportunity to get to know him better. After twenty minutes in his company he had concluded that he would always despise the man.

'They're rather late, but none the less most welcome.' Hugo's eyes lingered on Sylvie's lush figure swathed in rose silk. Her pearly hair was dressed at one side and a tumble of ringlets shimmered on to a delicate collarbone. 'God, she looks delectable,' Hugo muttered beneath his breath. Adopting a suave smile, he sauntered over to cordially greet them all.

'Go away!'

'You're not being very nice to me, and we both know that's not wise.' The veiled threat was purred through lips that still smiled, for Hugo was aware they were being observed. He looked across to where the ladies were grouped by the mantelpiece and gave Gloria Meredith a polite nod. 'I've been patient, but you have kept me waiting too long. It's time to finish what we started—you know you want to as much as do I.'

'You're insane! Let me pass,' Sylvie hissed and gave his chest an inconspicuous thump with the heel of a hand. She dodged to one side, but craftily he shifted his stance, blocking her way.

Hugo had managed to separate her from June and William whilst they were standing by the supper table. Then, with some subtle manoeuvring, he'd isolated her in a corner of the room close to the terrace. It was a warm evening and the large doors were half-open. Sylvie knew it was his intention to force her out into the darkness with him.

'You can't prefer that blockhead Vance to me.'

Frustration whined in his voice, making him sound like a petulant child.

'He is worth a dozen of you. Now let me pass or I shall make a scene.'

'I don't think you will. That would make me very angry and then I might go and find your lapdog again. If you won't tell me, perhaps it's time I persuaded Vance to explain why it is you like him so much.'

Sylvie's eyes raked the cruel face close to hers. 'Leave him alone. Do you hear me? If you do not, I shall—'

'You shall what, my love?' Hugo harshly whispered. 'Will you come and meet me, plead for him as you did before? I'll maim him tomorrow to make you do that.'

'You vile bully,' Sylvie choked. 'I would never meet you anywhere again. I swear if you don't leave us both be I'll tell my parents what you have done, what you threaten to do to me…'

Hugo looked down at her from his considerable height. His fingers dragged through his blond hair and for a moment he looked less cocksure. A grin restored his confidence. 'You won't say anything,' he muttered. He deliberately turned about, but his body was still a barrier to Sylvie's escape. 'You won't risk a scandal. Your father looks feebler than when last I saw him. Has he had another

attack? And as for your dear mama, she seems…
exceedingly nervous.' He glanced slyly down at
Sylvie. 'You wouldn't want to frighten the life out
of them and have it on your conscience.' A finger
touched Sylvie's cheek. She recoiled immediately
in disgust. 'Besides, your mother likes me. Make
her the happiest woman alive and agree to our betrothal. Do that, and I just might curb my impatience till our wedding night.'

A heavy leg nudged her hip as he attempted
to budge her on to the terrace. He yelped as
Sylvie ground her heel on to his instep in spir-
ited self-defence.

'You mustn't keep the lady all to yourself,
Hugo. It's bad manners.' Guy Markham tapped at
Hugo's arm, unperturbed by the snarl of annoyance that bared the younger man's teeth at the sudden interruption.

Guy politely held out an arm and Sylvie, with
a grateful smile, slipped past her tormentor and allowed Guy to escort her towards the buffet table.

'Something to eat?' Guy suggested gallantly.

'Thank you, no. I feel a little nauseated,' Sylvie
said with a faint smile.

Guy took a glance back at Hugo Robinson, who
was fanatically watching them. 'Fellow has the
same effect on me,' he said quietly.

Sylvie looked up at Guy and noticed the sympathy in his eyes. On impulse she said, 'Thank you for rescuing me. I cannot abide him, yet he has managed to make my mother think him charming and a good catch. Quite a feat for such a brute, would you not say?'

Guy grimaced agreement. 'He is certainly unpleasant. He was making fun of Janet earlier. He knows what I think of him.'

'He knows what *I* think of him too. Unfortunately, no well-earned insult penetrates that thick skull of his. He is such an arrogant oaf!'

Guy looked startled by Sylvie's vehemence. 'He is keen on you, you know. He told me so.'

Sylvie nodded despondently. 'I know. But I will never marry him. I suppose I must find someone, though.'

Guy cocked his head to look at her downcast face. 'You've plenty of time for that. Heavens! You're still a baby! I'd wager you're not yet eighteen.'

'I'm eighteen and a half and my mother is keen to get me wed before I…' She hesitated—she had no intention of letting slip the reason why her mother was now desperate to get her respectable. Guy was being kind, but she guessed even he would be repelled on knowing she had eloped, stayed the night at an inn with a man, then returned home still a spinster. 'I suppose it is what fond mothers and fathers want for their children: to see them settled, especially their daughters.' A little chuckle preceded her admitting, 'I have not always been as decorous as I might have been, as I'm sure you know.'

Guy grinned. 'I remember when you and your sisters would come over to Spire Park to play with Janet. You were always the one to be off climbing the trees for apples or shaking conkers out of branches. Always thought you a pretty girl, now you're a charmer too. Nice dress. Colour suits you.' Guy's spontaneous compliments made him blush and clear his throat.

Sylvie's smile radiated up at him and she murmured her thanks. She had not taken an awful lot of notice of Guy when they had visited Spire Park over the years. Now she regretted having missed the opportunity to have him as a friend. She thought she would probably have had more fun with him than with his sister. Janet had never been adventurous and disliked being outdoors. Sylvie imagined Guy must be a similar age to the Marquess of Rockingham and she had not thought Adam too old to be her friend. Now she feared they were anything but friends and she suffered an odd feeling of loss at knowing it.

When Adam had taken his leave of her family earlier in the week, he had said he was to return the following day to London. William had tried to persuade him to stay a while longer and take up the invitation to the Robinsons' soirée. Her parents had then added their voice to the encouragement, adding that they would be honoured if he would accept hospitality at Windrush. Adam had politely refused all offers. Sylvie knew his determination to quit Hertfordshire was not unconnected to the fact that he didn't want to see her again.

She disgusted him, not only because of her farcical elopement, but because she had made false accusations against him. Now she knew the truth about Lady Townsend and their relationship. She knew Adam had not lied, for she had asked William about the Marquess's brother.

Jake Townsend had been gravely wounded at Waterloo, William had told her. He had also confirmed, with a frown, that Jake was indeed married to a woman named Theresa. Sylvie had noticed then that William seemed alert to her impertinent interest, and so she had asked no more questions. Besides, she had learned enough to feel thoroughly ashamed of herself.

As though he had also been lost in introspection for the past few minutes, Guy suddenly blurted, 'I know I'm a bit older than you, and we haven't spoken in a while, but, if you seriously want to get married, *I*'ll marry you. Be honoured,' he announced, looking earnestly at Sylvie.

Sylvie gave him a smile and dipped her shiny blonde head in a gesture of gratitude. 'Why, that's very chivalrous of you, Mr Markham.' As his dazed look transformed to delight, she added quickly, 'But I fear that…well, I suppose I'm no different to most young ladies: it would be nice to at least try and find someone and fall in love.' A wistful look preceded her pragmatism. 'But if that doesn't work, well, I shall remember your kind offer,' she ended cheerfully.

'We've struck a deal, then,' Guy said, but looking a trifle deflated. 'I don't have a lot of luck with the ladies. Only said that to Rockingham the other day.'

'Whereas the Marquess, of course, seems popular in that respect,' Sylvie suggested.

'Oh, yes; nobody more sought after by the petticoat set.' Guy snorted a lewd laugh before he recalled to whom he was talking. He swung away his burning face and added, 'That is, I imagine…well Janet maintains he has a certain charisma. And of course he is handsome…I suppose…'

'I suppose,' Sylvie echoed with a wry inflection. 'You are handsome too,' she sweetly emphasised.

'I find it hard to believe that you are not already under siege from young ladies looking for a kind and decent man.'

Guy gave a modest tut, but his smile was broad. 'I was going back to London tomorrow, but I might just stay a few days longer. Shall we arrange to meet and go for a ride? And a picnic? Do you like fishing?'

'I do,' Sylvie told him. 'But you must return to London and I shall come and see you there. We can ride in Hyde Park at the fashionable hour and look for suitable people…people with whom we might fall in love.' She leaned conspiratorially close to him. 'I shall let you into a secret. My mama has been badgering me for ages to go to town and find a husband. Just yesterday I refused to go, but now…now I think I shall. Yes, I shall go to London because already I have a friend there. You. When June and William return to Mayfair, I shall go with them. And when June drags me off to Almack's to find an eligible man, you must come too. I could not bear the tedium if you weren't there. Promise me, Guy Markham, that you will come and dance with me…'

'Don't treat me like a fool! I'm a cripple, not brain sick.'

Adam turned from the window and watched as

his brother shifted his meagre weight to tilt more heavily on his ebony stick. Slowly Jake's frail body came over the rug towards him.

Adam watched his progress, feeling every laboured step rip into him, but he remained still. Even when Jake's withered limb buckled, and he stumbled and cursed, Adam curbed the instinct to rush forward and assist him. On more occasions than he cared to remember, he had been roughly pushed away when he tried to ease his only sibling's pain.

He watched Jake's face closely as he approached. Jake was younger by three years than he, but looked a decade older. He was still a handsome man, yet the years of mental and physical anguish had taken their toll. His once-muscular torso had wasted away and his sallow complexion held a constant grimace dug about his bloodless lips. But his eyes were alert and unrelenting.

'Where was she this time? And don't bother lying to protect my feelings, for she has no qualms about telling me herself should I care to ask.'

'Have you asked her?'

Jake laughed. It heaved from his sunken chest like a sob. 'I could not be bothered when first you brought her back. When I decided I might want to know, she had gone out. She was barely home long enough to change her clothes. She left a note to say she has gone to stay with her mother for a while. Apparently the old witch is ailing and Theresa's gone to Bristol to nurse her.' He took a fresh grip on his cane and found the strength to chuckle. 'She's taken precious little interest in tending to me over five years. Do you think she is really gone there?' The question hung in the air.

'Where did you find her? Who was she with?' Jake suddenly fired more questions at his brother.

Adam strode away from the window and five fingers forked through his long dark hair. 'What's the point in knowing? Does it matter who she was with this time?'

'Yes, dammit! She's my wife!' Jake screamed with such vehemence that his balance wobbled.

Adam sprang forward, but his brother tottered away from him and sank into an armchair.

'There is no need for you to tolerate this,' Adam enunciated with deadly calm. 'A divorce can be arranged…'

Jake sneered up at him. 'You'd like that, wouldn't you? Would it ease your conscience next time you bed her if she's no longer in my bed too?' A dry laugh cracked from his throat. 'Not that she is in mine often, of course.'

'I have no interest in your wife, Jake. How many times do I have to tell you that?'

'But she has a hell of an interest in you,' Jake spat. 'She makes that quite clear. Oh, she lets me know that she wants you back. She'll do anything to be your mistress again.'

Adam sank into the chair opposite and his head dropped into his hands. 'There is nothing she could do…'

On hearing Jake's shrill, lascivious laugh, Adam shouted, 'There is nothing she could do, I tell you. What was between us is finished. It is over and I wish to God I had never set eyes on the scheming harlot.' Adam looked across at his brother's livid face. 'Listen to me, she's no good, and you need to be rid of her before she makes of you a laughing stock.'

'Before *she* makes of me a laughing stock? I think you had a hand in achieving that when you bedded your sister-in-law whilst I was away fighting for King and country, don't you?'

'How many times do I have to tell you? She told me you were dead,' Adam ground out through touching teeth.

'How inconvenient of me to turn up alive and in this sorry state. Would you have married her had I perished?'

An abrupt, contemptuous noise was answer enough.

'No, of course you would not. Had you ever cared about her, you would never have passed her on to me all those years ago.'

'Nobody but a drunken fool would have considered marrying one of my cast-offs.'

Jake sank back in the chair and gave a despairing laugh. 'I was drunk and she was persuasive. There is not much a man can do in those circumstances.'

'You can do something about it now. Let me arrange a meeting with my attorney. You need not journey to the city; he would come here.'

'Don't make out that you are too shrewd and righteous to succumb to her tricks. She hooked you again as soon as I was out of the way. And you cuckolded your own brother,' Jake hissed malevolently. 'Whatever you say, I know she has not given up hope that when I die…'

'I'm sick of hearing your whining self-pity,' Adam suddenly roared. 'Why do you allow that poisonous bitch to continue to torment you? How many times do I have to say I'm sorry?' He sprang from the chair and headed for the door.

'Mother was here yesterday and asking after your whereabouts. I think she wants to see you.'

Jake's tone had become neutral. He withdrew a snuffbox from his pocket and leisurely took a pinch.

Adam brought under control his tense mind and body before curtly nodding. 'I'll go there now. I should have let her know I would be in the country for a few days.' Adam opened the door, but was arrested by his brother's voice.

'Who was she with?'

'Tobias Sheldon at the George and Dragon on the Great North Road,' Adam clipped out.

Jake sank back in his chair. '*Sheldon?*'

Adam could read in his face that Jake was surprised, perhaps even a little impressed, on discovering who had been his wife's latest conquest.

'Yes, I thought he had better taste too,' he said before closing the door quietly.

Chapter Ten

'How have you been?'

John nodded and muttered a response, but Sylvie could not clearly hear his words. The wind was strong, whipping at their faces and making their coats flap noisily. She guessed he had said that he was well enough, but she could sense a controlled sadness about him that plucked at her heart. Quickly she dismounted from Hazel and tethered the mare to a tree, seeking some shelter from the gusts. John urged his mount to follow her into the lee of the ancient oak.

The wind trembled a canopy of budding branches above Sylvie's head, making her shiver. As John dismounted and turned to her she hugged herself into her coat and took a penetrative look at his solemn expression. 'Are you still in bad trouble with your parents?' She guessed that might be causing his melancholy demeanour.

John shrugged and forced a smile.

'Are they angry that I wrote to you? Do they not want me to bother you?' The questions tumbled out.

Sylvie knew that since they returned home unwed their fathers had met by chance in the village on a few occasions. Her papa was reluctant to recount what had occurred between the two heads of family but, from snippets of overheard conversation between her parents, Sylvie had gleaned that a feud was fomenting between the Vances and Merediths. Loyalty to their children ensured both parties ostensibly held the other responsible for the fiasco.

She had not seen John once since that time. Sylvie had imagined he had bowed to his parents' insistence that he henceforth stay away from her bad influence. She had felt hurt by the thought of his defection, for just a short while ago they had been close enough friends to feel at ease eating and sleeping in the same room at the George and Dragon. As the days had dragged on, with no communication, it was almost as though their parents' hostility was infectious. An unspoken battle of wills seemed to have sprung up between them and only time would tell who first would yield and make contact.

Sylvie knew she could not contemplate going

for several months to London without first saying goodbye to the best friend she had ever had. She had thus swallowed her pride and written John a note asking him to meet her. Yesterday Frederick from Windrush's stables had taken her letter to the Vances' farm.

'They don't know about your note,' John eventually said. 'I was in the yard when Fred came. Besides,' he said, a trifle miffed, 'it is private between us and nothing to do with them.'

'They're still very angry, aren't they?' Sylvie stated quietly.

John simply nodded and thrust his hands into his pockets.

'I'm sorry, John,' Sylvie said with an emphatic gesture of regret. 'All of this is my fault. I did not want to cause you trouble. I should not have persuaded you to elope. You tried to tell me it would end badly, but I was too obstinate to take good advice—'

'I wanted to go as much as you,' John harshly interrupted. 'I wish we never had turned back.'

Sylvie's deep blue gaze roved his face at his unexpected forcefulness. 'At the time you seemed less determined to continue the journey.' She pointed out his failure to be decisive at that crucial time on the Great North Road.

John watched the toe of one of his scuffed boots grinding into peat. 'I wanted to go on, but I knew you had changed your mind. From the moment we met him at the George and Dragon, I knew…'

'Knew what?' Sylvie asked on a frown.

'I just knew…'

Sylvie adopted an impatient stance, hands on hips. 'What did you know, for Heaven's sake? Are you talking about Adam Townsend? What did you know about him?'

'I knew that he was the sort of man you suited. I know you deserve better than me, but I still wish we had gone on. You'd be my wife now and you'd be living with me at the farm.'

Sylvie pouted a sigh. 'If I'm truthful, perhaps that was one of the reasons I decided to turn back. I always liked your parents, but I'm not sure that Mrs John Vance and Mrs Frank Vance would thrive beneath the same roof.' She fondly gripped one of his arms with two hands. 'I wish we had not set out for Scotland, John, for then we would still be friends.'

'Aren't we still friends?' John asked, but his eyes had veered away to stare fixedly over her head. 'Hugo Robinson is over there by the brook. He is watching us.' He nodded his head towards the east.

Sylvie quickly turned about and squinted in that

direction. Horse and rider were quite still. Hugo must have known that he had been spotted, yet he made no move to ride on. Sylvie guessed his intention in staying put, and staring, was to intimidate them.

'Do you think he will come over?' There was a note of anxiety in John's voice that proved the success of Hugo's tactics.

Sylvie instinctively gave his arm a reassuring squeeze. 'You need not worry about that bully any more. He will not bother you once he finds out that I have gone to London.'

At John's sharp, enquiring look Sylvie explained, 'I have agreed to go to town with my sister and brother-in-law when they return home. My mother will not rest until I find myself a husband. I am quite ruined, you know,' she added wryly.

'There is no need for you to do that! We can still—'

Sylvie placed a quietening finger against his lips. Through a frown she smiled at him. 'It would not work, John. You tried to tell me when first I mentioned the stupid elopement that it was a mistake. But I can be selfish and silly; because you are my friend and want to please me, you tolerate it. I must change my ways or nobody will have me.' She glanced up at John, noticing his bewilderment and hurt. 'And you will find a wife who is worthy of being Mrs John Vance.'

'You mean I will find someone of my own station in life.'

'No!' Sylvie cried, but inside she cringed at his honesty and his perception. From the moment they had chanced upon Adam Townsend on the Great North Road, her resolve to marry John had wavered. Without consciously doing so, she had compared her rejected suitor to John…and found John wanting. Not that she loved him less; but now she understood her feelings would be the same for a longed-for and cherished brother. In her selfish way she had never properly considered John's needs, or that he might expect her to be a true wife who would provide him with children. How hopelessly selfish had been her plan that they would marry, but live together as friends! Now she understood why her first instinct had been to tell John not to be daft when he kissed her: it had made her feel awkward to be intimate in that way with him.

'He has gone,' John interrupted her guilt-ridden introspection.

Sylvie took a look to the east and saw Hugo riding away. 'It is our close friendship that feeds his resentment. He is so full of bombastic conceit that he cannot bear the fact that I hate him and like you.'

John wound the reins of his mount about a broad palm. 'I must get back. There is much to be done before supper.'

Sylvie nodded. 'I wish you well, John.'

'And I you,' he replied with an oblique smile for her.

Instinctively Sylvie enclosed him in a hard hug. 'I shall miss you!'

John stood motionless in that sweet embrace then slowly rested his chin on her silky crown of silver hair.

In the distance a rider reined in on the ridge of a hill. Man and beast were silhouetted, motionless, for several seconds against the horizon before plunging from view into the valley.

'Adam? At Almack's? I don't think so!' William guffawed at the very thought and wiped a mirthful tear from his eye.

June looked a trifle indignant. 'When he visited us at Windrush, he and Sylvie seemed…interested in each other. If he *is* attracted to her again, I thought he might make the effort to attend such a place.'

William gave his wife a wry smile. 'I think you're letting optimism get the better of you, my dear,' he said gently. 'My thoughts are that Rock-

ingham is content to remain a bachelor. But if
Sylvie is missing him, I can go to Upper Brook
Street and find out what he's been up to and where
you might track him down.'

'Don't you dare!' June warned crossly. 'It is for
him to seek *her* out. No sister of mine will ever be
desperate for a man's attention. He acknowledged
us on Monday as his curricle passed our coach in
Pall Mall, so he knows Sylvie is in town with me.
I have been expecting his card to arrive, but he has
not yet called on us at home. I thought, actually,
he seemed rather…distant.'

William cocked an eyebrow at his disgruntled
wife. 'And Sylvie? Is she feeling snubbed too?'

'She seems at pains to avoid mentioning him.
Which of course indicates that she is far from indifferent to Adam.'

William looked thoughtful at that. He had seen
Adam at his club just a few hours ago and, although they had passed the time of day, Adam had
indeed taken off when conversation turned to
June's family. A smile lifted a corner of his mouth.
Perhaps sweet Sylvie was again doing something
no other woman to his knowledge had managed:
getting under Adam Townsend's skin. It would be
interesting to find out. That thought prompted
William to say cheerily, 'Very well; if you are in-

tent on putting your sister in his way, I suggest we attend this one.' William selected a gilt-edged card from the marble mantelpiece and handed it to his wife. 'I was going to attend with my father. Lady Burdett is a close friend of Rockingham. If he is available, he is sure to attend her card party.'

June sent her husband a quelling look. William still seemed amused by the notion his friend might attend one of the assemblies held at Almack's that were haunted by débutantes stalking an eligible husband. With hindsight she realised it was idiotic to expect such a sought-after sophisticate to be tempted by insipid entertainment and lemonade. Defensively she said, 'I'm not sure that taking Sylvie to a salon hosted by Adam's mistress is a sensible idea.'

William shrugged. 'Just trying to be helpful, sweetheart,' he said with a fond grin. 'Besides, Deborah Burdett is not his mistress any more. But I know they are still amicable.'

Any further discussion on that lady's position in the Marquess's affections was abruptly curtailed as Sylvie entered the room. June gave her sister a bright smile. 'We were just saying, Sylvie, for a change you might like to play cards this evening. William will be going too. But I have vouchers for Almack's if you'd rather again go there.'

Sylvie gave a little mock shudder. 'I'd rather *not* again go there.' She took the invitation. Having scanned the elegant script, she returned it with a winsome smile. 'Yes, if you like, let's play cards. I don't mind.'

'Well, that's settled, then.' June replaced the card on the mantelpiece with a subdued sigh. Despite her best efforts to keep Sylvie entertained, her sister already seemed homesick and bored with the social whirl. It was poignantly obvious that Sylvie was curbing her rebellious nature and trying to placate their mother after halfworrying her to death. Sylvie was proving her remorse, and how much she loved their parents, by gamely persevering in the role of decorous young lady simply to lure a husband she did not want. June felt saddened by her plight; there was so much more to marriage than finding a stranger who would let you live with him.

June watched as Sylvie seated herself, then idly flicked over pages in a fashion journal. Her eyes darted from page to window to door. She was preoccupied, that was obvious, and June wondered whether memories of John Vance were causing her distraction.

Sylvie closed the book and went to the window. She peered out into the dismal afternoon. A fine misty rain was clogging the skies and shrouding the street scene in grey gloom. She sighed. She had been in town for almost a week and was already yearning to be back at Windrush. She did not suit town life. She had made few friends amongst the giggling young ladies who, like her, were being chaperoned to the most exclusive balls and assemblies in the hope they might tempt an eligible man to offer for them.

Not that she had been wholly unsuccessful in that respect. So far Sir Alan Montague and Mr Stephen Shepherd had made it clear they liked her very much. Neither gentleman had stirred in her any stronger sentiments than her acknowledging that they weren't unpleasant. So Sylvie had charmingly damped down their ardour without implying all hope was lost. She knew she must find a husband, but, so far, of all the gentlemen who had seemed willing to take on the role, Guy Markham was her favourite. Yet she had seen nothing of him. William's opinion on his absence was that the poor fellow must have been delayed in Hertfordshire, caught up in his duties as chief usher at his sister's approaching wedding.

'Is Guy Markham yet arrived in town?'

'He was at White's earlier,' William volunteered. 'He asked after you, Sylvie. He said he was looking forward to seeing you. I believe he might go to Lady Burdett's.'

Sylvie beamed. 'Oh, we must definitely go then!'

June and William exchanged a look. The news of Guy's arrival had at last extracted some enthusiasm from Sylvie. 'I hadn't realised that his presence would buck you up so much.' June gave Sylvie an arch look; it prompted her sister to respond by idly twirling a pearly ringlet about a finger.

'Guy has promised to take me for a drive in Hyde Park, and when next we do go to dreary Almack's I know he will come and keep me entertained.'

'You were hardly lacking for partners, Sylvie,' June pointed out. 'Your card was full within fifteen minutes of our arrival.'

Sylvie grimaced. 'I'd sooner have partnered Guy at every dance. He's better company than any of those primped fops.'

'No more than two dances with any one gentleman is the general rule. No more scandalous behaviour, if you please,' June said severely but ruined the reprimand by laughing. 'Besides, I thought you liked Mr Shepherd.'

'I'd like him better if he didn't smear rouge on his lips.'

'Sir Alan Montague?' June enquired.

'He uses tongs to style his hair.'

'How do you know that?' June asked on a gurgle of laughter.

'His coiffure was distinctly frizzled in places and I thought I ought mention it. We ended up discussing the best size of irons to use so as not to singe a curl.'

'I think I ought retire to my study. I need to recuperate for this evening, or I might lose a fortune,' William interrupted, before breaking into laughter. 'I know Sir Alan is due to go to Lady Burdett's party. He plays a mean hand of faro, no matter the state of his toupee.'

He was ignoring them and making it quite obvious too!

Sylvie took a little glance at June, noticing that she looked distinctly pink about the cheeks as she peeked over her shoulder to where the group of gentlemen stood on the terrace. Her sister was equally conscious of the lack of warmth in the brief greeting they'd received.

Anger bubbled up in Sylvie. The Marquess of Rockingham might not like *her*, but he had no business turning his back on her sister! Had June not done him the great honour of asking him to be godfather to her firstborn? Had her family not recently treated him hospitably when he visited Windrush? How dare he act so high and mighty!

Sylvie looked swiftly about for William and noticed he was just seating himself with his father, Alexander Pemberton, at the whist table.

Linking arms with June, Sylvie urged her away from the double doors that led outside—where the unmannerly Marquess was grouped with some of his noisy cronies—and towards the baize-covered table at which William was seated.

'Why do you not partner William?' Sylvie said gaily. 'I have just noticed that one of the young ladies I met at Almack's is here with her mother. And I think that is her fiancé hovering close by. I must go and have a cose and see what I think of him, for she is very nice.'

In order not to seem to be deceitful, Sylvie did stop for a few moments next to Lucy Carstairs. She even cooed over her magnificent diamond ring for a second before slipping away towards the terrace.

Chapter Eleven

'I should like to speak to you.'

Adam turned his head, still laughing, and looked down into a pair of enchanting eyes glaring at him. Another gentleman also reacted to that curt command, eying the irate blonde beauty with lusty interest before giving Adam a subtle wink.

Adam gave him a blatant scowl before he stepped away from his group of friends. A hard hand manacled a soft arm and he propelled Sylvie along the terrace to an area where they might be private.

'Have you never learned any manners?'

Sylvie was unperturbed by that scathing reprimand. She wrenched her wrist from captivity as a contemptuous little laugh burst from her. 'How odd! I was about to ask you the very same thing.'

Adam forced his eyes away from the small

bosom straining furiously against silk. Her nipples were closing into buds beneath the caress of the cool evening air and his hand was responsively curving. Abruptly he jammed his palm on to the iron balustrade. The other fingers were kept busy dispensing ash on to stone flags. Irritably he tossed away the glowing cigar stub to trace an arc on the darkness. 'I'm not about to show any interest in why you think me rude. Go back inside.'

'That doesn't signify. I'm about to tell you anyway. And don't order me about.'

'Why not? You order me about. Come here…go there…stay…leave…don't touch…'

Sylvie gazed up at a profile that might have been carved in stone. He swung his head and molten eyes flowed over her mutinous face. She swallowed and crossed her arms over her middle. 'I know we don't get on, but at least have the decency to spare June a few minutes of your precious time instead of so briefly speaking to her. It's not her fault she is my sister. She and William have bestowed on you the honour of being godfather to Jacob. I have to admit I was surprised by their choice.'

'I'd be surprised if you weren't. You've made it clear you don't hold me in high esteem.'

Sylvie glowered at him and tossed platinum curls back from her youthful features. 'Our mutual disregard is not important. Why are you slighting June? She thinks of you as her friend.'

'And I am.'

'Then why are you—?'

'For God's sake!'

The imprecation was blasted out through gritted teeth, startling Sylvie into a silent, wary stare.

'Do you understand who I am?' he asked with a deceitfully honeyed tone that made her heart jump a beat.

Sylvie simply nodded.

'I don't think you do. I am the Marquess of Rockingham. I am thirty-three years old and I do not justify my behaviour to anyone, least of all to an impudent child who should be home in bed instead of plaguing me. What in damnation are you doing in London in any case?'

'As you don't feel obliged to give explanations, neither do I.' Sylvie took a provocatively long look at a set of neat fingernails.

'Humour me, please,' he suggested gently, 'before I do something I really should not.'

Sylvie stabbed startled eyes at his face at that caution. 'What will you do?' she demanded. The suspicion that he might betray her secret, here in such company, again made her heart beat erratically. She clutched at his arm, steady on the railing, and shook it. 'You would not tell…not here. Even you would not be so vile as to do that!'

Adam gave a grim laugh and prised the ferocious grip from his forearm. Sylvie endeavoured to snatch back her hand, but he refused to release it. 'No; even I would not be so vile as to do that,' he agreed sarcastically. 'But if you do not inform me why you are in town, I shall be sorely tempted to treat you like the brat you are and put you across my knee. Unfortunately I am vile enough to do that.'

Sylvie shrank back, renewing her efforts to liberate herself from his clutches. He looked strict enough to carry out the threat.

His lips mockingly saluted her wriggling fingers before he let her go.

Sylvie backed against the railing and planted a hand either side of her. Her instinct was to cravenly bolt back inside, but she forced herself to be still. 'I'm not frightened of you,' she quavered. 'Don't try to bully me or I shall hit you back. I've hit a man before and he didn't like it!'

Adam watched her chin tilt beneath his steady regard. For all her fierce pride and independence he could see her lower lip was under attack from small teeth and the knuckles on the balustrade were showing bone. His eyes closed in self-disgust for still the frustrated desire in him lingered. He stared off into the night and said quietly, 'You infuriate me into saying things I don't mean. I wouldn't hurt you. Who has?'

Quickly she pushed forward and dodged to pass him, regretting her unguarded comment. 'I simply wanted to tell you I thought you have been unkind to June,' she murmured.

He moved as she did and blocked her way. 'I'm sorry if your sister thinks I've been aloof. I would not consciously offend any member of your family.'

'Apart from me.'

'I don't want to offend you…or to antagonise you. I admit I do it, but then you started it.' A half-smile touched his mouth as she immediately dipped her face in abashed acknowledgement of that truth. 'I should like us to be more harmonious, Sylvie.'

'Harmonious?' Sylvie tested the word.

'Yes,' he said huskily, whilst in his mind he mocked himself for a pathetic fool. He tolerated too much from this angelic chit. Apart from his brother, nobody dared speak to him the way she did. Not his friends, his peers or his lovers. Even his mother, who had some right to check his conduct, was assiduously diplomatic with her opinion. Nobody at all laid angry hands on him. This little vixen was wont to pummel him, yet her touch was as welcome as a mistress's caress.

She seemed unspoiled, despite having a lover, and the anomaly tormented him. Even when he had sat with his brother and talked of the wanton Jake had married, the woman bothering him was this one.

He had property on several continents worth more than a million pounds and an equal sum in the bank, yet he found himself considering how fortunate could be a modest tenant farmer. He was respected and admired by friends and acquaintances for his cool composure, yet felt tempted to lash out in a jealous rage because the woman with whom he'd been prepared to share his life and riches preferred being kissed by someone else. Someone with very little…but perhaps Vance had all he needed. And no matter what roistering pleasure he plunged into, he could not convince himself that only his ego had suffered from knowing any of it.

To further injure his pride, he now knew that his sulking had not gone unnoticed. He had betrayed his weakness and appeared discourteous to people he liked and classed as friends.

'It would be nice if we stopped arguing.' Sylvie's soft voice splintered the protracted quiet. She accepted the proffered olive branch and sweetly returned the gesture. 'As you have said sorry for something, then so must I.'

She frowned at her gripped fingers while trying to regiment jumbled words in her mind. For her conscience's sake she must apologise for having readily concluded that vice had taken him to a tavern on the fateful night he'd caught John and her masquerading as man and wife. 'When we met you at the George and Dragon, I should not have assumed that the lady you were with was a…that is to say, I should not have been rude about your sister-in-law.' She could have said more about the horrible way the woman had humiliated her own husband, but she didn't want to sound self-righteous. Her own behaviour at that time had hardly been blameless.

Sylvie took a wary glance at Adam, but could read little emotion in his profile. 'Are your brother's injuries very bad?' she probed in a hushed voice.

'Yes, they are,' Adam answered quietly while still gazing impassively into darkness. 'Jake has difficulty walking and has lost sensation and muscle in his right leg. He cannot take exercise and his body is weakening. The shrapnel hit his chest, too, close to his heart. Although that wound started to close quite quickly it became poisoned and he was not expected to survive the journey back from the Peninsula. In fact, at one time, I heard he had died.'

Sylvie's huge eyes glistened with sympathy. 'Perhaps there is a doctor somewhere who might be able to help him.' She had spoken spontaneously and immediately felt foolish. The Marquess of Rockingham obviously cared greatly for his brother, Jake. Why would he journey miles north to bring home the man's wayward wife, if not to spare him the humiliation of being a cuckold? Adam would have already investigated every possible way of easing his physical pain. 'I expect you know what the medical profession have to offer,' she corrected herself a trifle self-consciously.

Adam gave Sylvie a slanted smile. 'I think more than ten have examined him. Some have promised miracle cures, others that they would simply do their best. Jake has been pulled and pummelled and has swallowed all manner of pills and potions. Now he refuses any more of it and calls them all quacks and charlatans.' Adam looked bleakly off into space. He knew that in a way Jake didn't really want to improve, for his poor, disfigured body was a constant symbol of the bitterness that lay between them: it was more a stick with which to beat him than that ebony cane that kept him upright.

'Sometimes something simple is quite efficacious. My sister Isabel is very good with potions and cures. I recall once, when Isabel lived in York with Aunt Florence, that a little lad fell off the water wheel at Kirby Mill. His arm was terribly mangled. Isabel mixed some rubbing oils and used them on the boy when the doctors could offer him no more. She persevered with the massage and, though he was not perfect by any means, he regained the use of that arm and astonished everyone.'

She watched Adam's face, hoping for a reaction. 'Surely something like that is worth a try? Shall I write and ask her advice?'

Adam swung his head around to gaze at the pure concern on Sylvie's face. A wave of such tenderness swept over him that it rocked him to the balls of his feet. This sweet child cared more for Jake's health and happiness, without having ever spoken to him, than did the man's own wife. He knew that Jake would refuse all offers of help, probably in forceful terms punctuated with foul oaths, but he muttered huskily, 'Thank you for that, Sylvie. You're very kind.'

Sylvie smiled modestly. 'I'll do it tomorrow. I know Isabel is preparing a poultice for Sir Anthony's bad leg.' Aware of those dark eyes fixed on her face, she turned about and gazed off into the darkness. 'It is uncommonly warm for so early in the year.'

Adam mirrored her pose, leaning on the railing

and pondering the night sky. 'It has certainly been fine weather,' he continued the light dialogue.

After a few minutes of companionable quiet, Sylvie sighed regretfully. 'I suppose I must go back inside. June will wonder where on earth I am.'

The soft words drifted into his consciousness, drawing his eyes from the stars studded into the horizon. His hands dove into his pockets as he said, 'Do you know how to play gin rummy?'

Sylvie caught her bottom lip between her teeth and, with a sweetly shy smile, shook her head.

Adam held out his arm; without hesitation, Sylvie placed small fingers on his immaculate sleeve.

His palm slid slowly to cover her skin, warm and caressing, in a way that made her slant questioning eyes to his.

'It's time you learned,' he said.

'How do I look?' Sylvie did a little pirouette in front of her sister and the pretty morning dress swirled about her shapely calves and ankles.

June cocked a judicious eye at her. 'It is surprising that primrose colour becomes you as your hair is so fair. It looks very nice…stylish, yet demure,' she added with a smile. 'Heavens, Sylvie! I never thought I would see the day when I described you as demure.' She glanced at the clock. 'What time is Guy calling for you?'

'Four-thirty.' They were in the small salon that was situated on the first floor of Grove House, the Pembertons' elegant mansion in St James's. Sylvie stepped to the lofty window and peered down into the street.

Today she felt light-hearted, quite happy to be in town with her sister and brother-in-law. She knew that her good humour was not unconnected to the fact that Adam and her seemed to be under truce.

He had not stayed long at her side last evening. Once he had kept to his word and instructed her how to play gin rummy—and allowed her to win a half-sovereign from him—he had made his excuses and left. Sylvie had noticed that their hostess, Lady Burdett, looked rather crestfallen at his early departure. Sylvie had felt oddly bereft too, but her admirers—Guy included in their number— had kept her entertained as they vied good-naturedly for her to partner them at cards, or for the privilege to collect her drinks or titbits from the buffet.

The antagonism between Adam and her was waning and that knowledge had settled on Sylvie a sense of serenity and security. She had expected he might again demand to know why she was in town, but he seemed to have accepted that she had simply returned with June and William as their guest.

As they had been leaving the card party, Guy had asked if he might visit the following day and take her for a drive. The most devoted of her admirers was still loitering in her vicinity and had, unfortunately, heard Guy's request granted. Mr Shepherd had looked rather forlorn for, some moments beforehand, she had gently rebuffed his entreaty to be permitted to pay a call. Sylvie had felt rather guilty as she watched him trudge disconsolately away.

Her eyes focused again on the street just as a phaeton hove into view, then came bowling along at quite a crack. Sylvie smiled in delight as she saw the high-flyer so expertly tooled. 'Here is Guy now,' she told June over her shoulder.

'Tea would be most acceptable,' Guy responded to June's hospitality with a wide smile.

June went to summon a servant to bring it and her guest turned his attention to Sylvie. 'If I remember correctly, we are soon to head for the Park and look for suitable people with whom we might form an attachment.'

Sylvie gave him a mischievous smile. 'Indeed we are, sir; you have a fine memory. And I wish you had arrived in town earlier in the week so we might have already started our quest. That way, perhaps by now I might have met my perfect match and could let Mr Shepherd know the cause is lost.'

'Is he making a nuisance of himself?' Guy asked with a frown. He expanded his chest, dropped his voice an octave. 'You only have to say the word and I shall teach him some manners that he won't forget.'

'No! It's not that at all.' Sylvie, in alarm, quickly protected her admirer. 'I find him quite amusing, even though I am not sure he intends to be. He is always polite, if a little too…ardent with his compliments.' Sylvie gave an emphatic nod. 'No, Mr Shepherd is not an unpleasant gentleman at all.'

Guy was still striking a manful pose, but eventually relinquished it to take his tea and accept the invitation to sit down.

'Are the wedding plans going well?' June asked conversationally as she joined her sister on the sofa. 'We supposed that those preparations must have caused you to delay your return to town.'

Guy, with a frown suddenly corrugating his brow, was on the point of answering when Herbert, the Pembertons' butler, materialised in the doorway. In a hushed tone, that betrayed his deference, he announced, 'The Marquess of Rockingham is here, ma'am.'

June put down her cup and jumped to her feet. 'Please show him up, Herbert,' she instructed eagerly.

Guy consulted his watch with a grin. 'He's cutting it fine if he still hopes to journey into Surrey. He said yesterday he was going to the races today.'

Sylvie felt an odd little *frisson* at the news of Adam's impromptu arrival. They had parted on good terms, yet it seemed that sometimes, out of nowhere, friction could instantly flare between them. She didn't want that to happen. She hoped their truce would last.

Both June and Guy looked pleased that Adam had arrived. Despite the rumours of his licentious lifestyle, it seemed the Marquess of Rockingham was welcomed everywhere. Sylvie recalled that Guy had revealed—then looked mortified to have done so—that Adam was *sought after by the petticoat set*. He had not needed to fret over offending her delicate sensibilities; at the age of sixteen Sylvie had overheard a conversation in which it was mentioned that demi-reps vied for Adam's company. Now older and wiser, she accepted it had been outrageously impertinent of her to ask the gentlemen what was a demi-rep. A *lady of doubtful character* had been her answer, given to her by the Earl of Malvern himself while her poor papa had looked fit to explode with embarrassment. In her shocking naïvety she had imagined *she* might be a demi-rep. It had been, she again reassured herself, a logical assumption for a sixteen-year-old to make; had she not been warned time and again by her weary mother that she would *suffer consequences* should she not improve her behaviour?

Suddenly, as Sylvie observed Adam warmly greeting June, a wistful thought came upon her that it might have been very nice had they met again under better circumstances than those fate had foisted on them at the George and Dragon.

Adam accepted June's invitation to be seated and chose to sit down next to Sylvie on the small sofa.

June gave Adam his tea, then settled down close to Guy for an animated chat about the vital nature of a chief usher's duties.

Adam leaned forward and deposited his cup and saucer on a table. 'Would you like to go for a drive?'

Sylvie turned to him and smiled. 'In your curricle?'

'Yes.'

Instinctively a disappointed sigh escaped her. 'I can't. Guy has already kindly asked me to go out with him. And it would be rather a squash if we all went together in either the curricle or the phaeton.'

'Heaven forbid we should try it,' Adam said with a grimace of mock alarm. His dark eyes roved her face, dropped to take in the elegant cut of her clothes. 'The first time I saw you I thought you looked like a grubby goddess…all shaggy blonde curls and dirty dress.'

Sylvie smoothed her skirt and tried to appear nonchalant despite the fact she could feel a blush rising in her cheeks. 'That was a long time ago. I expect I had been potting in the garden. I like being outdoors,' she explained defensively.

'It wasn't that long ago,' Adam countered. 'I recall being amazed when June told me that you were then almost seventeen.'

Sylvie's lips slanted to a defiant line. 'Earlier I was thinking how nice it would be if our truce could last a while yet.'

'And now?' Adam asked with laughter in his tone.

'And now…I think we ought change the subject or it certainly will not.'

Adam shrugged wry defeat and leaned back into the sofa. The fact that he could now observe her from behind made Sylvie drop her eyes down, then to one side, then twist about to face him.

His eyes held hers, smouldering amusement far back in their earthy depths. 'I wasn't complaining. I liked that grubby goddess.'

'Why?'

She could tell that he hadn't expected that question. She sat back, so they were once again levelly facing each other, and crossed her arms over her waist. 'Tell me why the grand Adam Townsend, who is so popular with the ladies, should have taken to a girl of sixteen who had shaggy hair and a dirty dress.'

He ignored the question and asked one of his own. 'Who told you I'm popular with the ladies?'

Sylvie huffed a little laugh. 'Nobody had to tell me. I worked that out for myself some while ago.'

'Indeed? And how did you account for my appeal?'

Sylvie's shrug, coupled with her expression, hinted at saucy insolence, but she refrained from saying she found it a mystifying enigma. 'Guy's sister thinks you have charisma, Guy told me.'

Adam's eyes slew to his friend and a sardonic tilt to his mouth told Sylvie he was not necessarily pleased on knowing he had been under discussion.

'What a charming idea,' he said softly. 'Alas, I think my bank balance holds more allure than I do.'

'Are you very rich?'

'Very.'

Sylvie nodded. 'You ought to have attracted a wife then,' she emphasised. 'Did you not propose to anyone else?'

'What? And face the humiliation of another rejection?'

She pretended ignorance of his dulcet irony. 'I doubt you would have been rejected. After all, you have a title as well as lots of money.'

'Those things didn't sway you.'

'Yes, but I was young and silly when you asked. I didn't realise then just what I was do—' Sylvie quickly sat forward and picked up his tea. 'This will get cold,' she said. 'You ought drink it.'

'Do you regret turning me down?' He took the cup and saucer from her and placed it back on the table.

'Of course,' she said brightly. 'You have lots of money and a title. I would be a fool not to regret it. And you are a charismatic gentleman who is popular with the ladies. I should like to be envied for my husband as my sisters are for theirs.'

'I get the distinct impression that you have had a lovers' tiff with John Vance. Is that why you have come to town? To teach him a lesson?'

He had spoken quietly, but none the less Sylvie took a wary glance at June and was relieved to see she was still deep in conversation with Guy. Sylvie shook her head with extreme brevity. 'No…we didn't argue,' she murmured. 'But I don't think his parents like me any more.' She picked up her tea-cup and sipped. 'I'm glad you came to see June this afternoon. She will be reassured now that she has not upset you.'

'Have you told her that it is you who have been upsetting me?'

Adam seemed infuriatingly determined to pursue a conversation Sylvie did not want. In a low voice she warned, 'Nobody in my family knows that you witnessed our elopement. If June were aware of it…' Sylvie flicked an eloquent hand. 'Naturally she would be mortified to think you knew about something so…scandalous. She might pack me off home, then I would never find a husband.'

The ensuing silence seemed interminable. Finally Adam said, 'You're looking for a husband?'

Sylvie nodded. 'I must, because if it ever should come to light that I ran away with John…well, I need not explain further. You know very well what occurred, and what the certain outcome would be.'

'What of John Vance? Is he happy about this?'

Sylvie shook her head, sending silky tresses rippling about her shoulders. 'No. He is not happy,' she whispered with the guilt strong in her voice. 'But I think…I hope…he understands that… Oh, please let us not talk of it any more,' she implored softly whilst glancing at her sister. This time she noticed that June was indeed shooting curious looks at the sofa.

'So I am to have a ride in your curricle at last,' Sylvie gaily said to Adam. 'You must point out any eligible gentlemen that we pass. Guy has promised to do that for me when we take a ride in his phaeton.'

'Is that all that matters? That a future husband is eligible? You're not interested in what sort of man he might be?'

'Of course I should like more than that. I should like someone who is…' Sylvie drifted into quiet and her eyes shadowed dreamily as she wistfully acknowledged her yearning.

From far away she heard him prompt her for an answer.

She shrugged herself back into consciousness. 'Oh, I don't know…someone like you, I suppose.'

Chapter Twelve

'Is that a marriage proposal?'

It was impossible for Sylvie to retaliate with a flippant rejoinder. Despite having told Adam quite recently that she would not marry him should he drop to his knees and beg her to do so, there was nobody she would rather call her husband. She slipped a glance at him from beneath her lashes and inwardly winced at his mockery. To him she was still that grubby girl: a quaint chit who had given a fillip to his jaded fancy. She rather thought that, if he knew how painfully honest had been her unguarded comment, he might look less languidly amused by it all and discover a reason to leave.

'What I meant was that I should like…' She searched her mind for something about him that was impersonally attractive. 'I should like an amiable mother-in-law, of course. I think that is important. For a long time June did not get along with her mother-in-law and it made her miserable. But now they are friends. I recall meeting your mother and thinking that she was nice to me.'

'And I recollect that she said to me she found you quite charming. I believe I told her that I was similarly smitten…'

Adam's intimate tone made blood pound beneath her ribs. This, then, was how a practised flirt made conquests. Oh, she could understand why this man was popular with the ladies. Should he stir himself to bother, she imagined he could have any woman he wanted.

'I might settle for Guy Markham. I like him. And his mother is quite pleasant.' Sylvie's voice was husky with forced nonchalance.

'Does he know?' Adam asked drily.

'That I like him? I think so.'

'That you might settle for him,' Adam corrected.

'Oh, yes, I told him that when he asked me to marry him.'

'Guy Markham has asked you to marry him?' A slow and steady look was directed at Guy's profile.

When, from the corner of an eye, Guy became aware of that searing observation, it prompted him to bounce to his feet.

'We ought hurry and set off, Miss Sylvie,' Guy warned. 'We'll miss the fashionable set on parade. Expect we're lagging behind the other young ladies doing Park sorties. That won't do! Won't do at all.'

''Tis not my fault we have yet to take a drive together, Mr Markham,' Sylvie softly teased Guy as she stood up. 'Had you arrived in town when you said you would, we might be leading the field in pursuit of several fine fellows.'

'I wish I *had* got here sooner. Wasn't happily delayed in Hertfordshire, you know!' Guy's demeanour was sombre. 'Wasn't Janet's wedding plans kept me there, I can tell you!' Guy shook his head, propped his chin on a fist, making ready to tell his tale. 'A fellow was waylaid one evening and attacked. I volunteered to help some other local men try to apprehend the thieving cur who did it.' He hissed an emphatic whistle through his teeth. 'It might have been more than one person who set about him, for young Vance's injuries were bad. Somebody mentioned that undesirables had been reported loitering close to the Cambridge road. But no sign of anyone up to no good.'

From the moment John's name had registered in her mind, Sylvie fought to comprehend what ensued. She still stared at Guy, watched his lips form words, but felt she had been isolated in an icy fog that numbed her senses.

'Despite their years, Frank Vance and Edgar Meredith joined in the search.'

The sound of her papa's name broke Sylvie's daze.

'The investigation is to continue, but I expect the culprit is far away by now,' Guy concluded his woeful tale.

Sylvie tore her eyes from Guy's face just as her sister enveloped her in a comforting embrace.

'Harrowing tale. Should not have recounted it,' Guy whispered to Adam who, now lithely on his feet, was looking gravely thoughtful. 'Miss Sylvie looks terribly wan.' Apology and concern throbbed in Guy's voice.

Sensitive to her guest's abashment, June informed quietly, 'John Vance is a particular friend of Sylvie's. It is such a terrible thing to happen and has come as a shock.'

'Is he…is John now recovering?' Sylvie gasped that question out as she withdrew from her sister's arms. Her throat felt constricted with a wedge of horrified suspicion. Was she alone in suspecting who had subjected John to such brutality? Of course she was! The only other person who could point a finger of blame was the victim, and he was badly wounded. 'Is John now better?' she demanded.

'He was…unconscious still when I left Hertfordshire. The physician had attended him,' Guy quickly added, trying to instil optimism into his tone. 'I'm sure he will recover and give a description of his attacker.'

Oh, John, please get well. He has beaten you senseless, perhaps tried to kill you, so you don't expose him for the fiend he is. The prayer for her friend sighed silently through her mind.

'I shall go to my room for a while,' Sylvie informed them all in a sob-like breath as she backed towards the door. Her eyes fleetingly clung to Adam's steady stare before her sister took her attention.

'Please, June, I would be alone for a while.' With that hoarse excuse flying in her wake, Sylvie avoided her sister's outstretched arms and turned and fled.

The soft tapping at the door became louder and more insistent. 'Open the door, Sylvie,' June called. 'I'm worried about you. You have been shut in there for a whole day. Here, I have brought you some tea…please let me in.'

Sylvie rubbed her hot, red-rimmed eyes against

the pillow to dry them, then dragged her weep-wearied body to the edge of the bed. Some of the crumples in her dress were dislodged by a twitch of a hand as she went to unlock the chamber door.

'I have to go home to Windrush,' Sylvie announced in despair as soon as June stepped into the room and put down the tea tray.

'There is nothing you can do, Sylvie!' June softly emphasised. 'You would simply further distress yourself if you were not allowed to see John. I don't think his parents got over the trouble of the elopement…now this.' She sighed before coaxing, 'Why do you not wait till we have more news from Hertfordshire? I'm sure that John will soon be on the mend. Perhaps by then the authorities will have some success with their investigations too.'

A bitter laugh interrupted June's reassurances. 'They are wasting their time looking for him. That devil will have covered his tracks too well.'

'You can't be sure of that, Sylvie.' June desperately sought to give solace to her sister. 'The vile coward who did this was probably more interested in fleeing with the coins he stole.' At Sylvie's enquiring frown, June explained, 'Guy told me, just as he and Adam were leaving here yesterday, that John was beaten for the few crowns he carried in his pocket. Frank Vance recalled that John had set out for town to collect provisions from Barton's store. He never reached his destination and that money was missing when they found him by the roadside.'

'Perhaps the coins were taken to make it seem theft was the motive,' Sylvie voiced querulously.

June looked bewildered. 'But why would anyone want to hurt John? He has always seemed to me to be a fairly mild-mannered chap. I would not have thought he had enemies to speak of.'

At Sylvie's silence, June's observation became more probing. 'Do you know if he has enemies, Sylvie?'

Sylvie's face dropped into her palms. Nobody knew of the vendetta Hugo Robinson had waged against John and her. The last time John was beaten by the bully, his injuries had been explained away to his parents as a fall from his horse. John had lied to protect her, for Hugo had taunted John that he would make her suffer if he was betrayed. But concealment had been in vain for he had hurt her anyway, because *she* had been trying to protect John from *him*.

She had not confided to a soul the humiliation she had suffered at Hugo's hands. Even June, the sister to whom she had always been closest, was ignorant of why she hated their neighbour's son.

Sylvie had, at times, yearned to unburden herself, but she hesitated because of the trust and loyalty that bound June and William. They refused to keep secrets from each other, and if William were to be apprised of the abuse his sister-in-law had suffered he would never let such an outrage go unpunished.

It would end in heartache, for her papa was susceptible to another attack if agitated, and her poor mama would not cope with knowing details of the indignities that had been meted out to her youngest child. Neither of them would want the inquisitiveness and malicious gossip that would follow the scandal. Oddly, Sylvie did not want Sir Anthony and Lady Robinson to be tainted by their son's depravity either. She liked them both, despite the abomination they had spawned. And then there was the niggling guilt that wormed into her conscience. Was there a grain of truth in Hugo's defence of his brutality? Had her wild behaviour been a reprehensible incitement to lechery?

June's hand on her arm drew Sylvie's anguished pensiveness to a halt. 'Do you suspect somebody, Sylvie?' June asked in a hushed voice.

Sylvie quickly shook her head.

June sighed in relief and went to pour tea. 'I am supposed to attend Lady Forster's salon this afternoon, but I have no taste for socialising. I think I will send a note conveying my excuses. I'd rather stay here with you…'

'You must go,' Sylvie interrupted and endorsed that with a wan smile. 'I would sooner be morose on my own. Perhaps I will go to the nursery and play with Jacob to cheer myself up.'

Now June summoned up a weak smile. 'The poor little mite is suffering still with his teeth, but might brighten on seeing you. I shall not stay long at Lady Forster's. I hate to leave him when he is fretful.'

A light tap on the door broke Sylvie's catnap. Gently she laid her drowsy nephew back in his cot, positioned close to her comfy chair. She reluctantly pushed away from the cushions and gained her feet as Molly entered the nursery. The young woman announced in a whisper, as her eyes lingered on the dozing infant, 'There's a gentleman below, miss, as would beg leave to see you.'

'Who is it, Molly?' Sylvie's fingers clenched in trepidation—immediately she suspected Guy might have returned with more news from Hertfordshire. Perhaps it was dreadful news…

The young woman looked reflective as she tried to recollect the name the butler had told her to convey. 'A…Mr Hugo Robinson…I think Mr Herbert said, miss.'

The name caused Sylvie to visibly flinch and the maid goggled anxiously at her. 'Are you all right, miss?'

Sylvie nodded whilst in her mind whirled feverish thoughts. Her first instinct was to send him away. The idea of being in the same room as Hugo Robinson made her feel bilious, but… She had, as yet, no proof that Hugo had anything to do with John's injuries. She was stunned as much to know Hugo was in town as to know he had the gall to come and call on her. Perhaps he had been in London some while and thus had an alibi for the vicious crime she was keen to lay at his door. She slid a look at Molly, who had been watching her whilst she paced, cogitating, back and forth. An opportunity had presented itself to discover the truth and she must steel herself to use it, for John's sake.

'Tell Herbert I will be down shortly, please, Molly.'

Once back in her own chamber, Sylvie sank to the edge of the bed with bowed head. Again she was assailed by images of John's battered face. Once before she had seen him bruised and bleeding and, on that occasion, there was no mystery as to who was the guilty party. Suddenly she was convinced the vile beast waiting below had come to torment her with what he had again done, safe in the knowledge that she would be intimidated into silence. Her memory pounced on his threats at the Robinsons' soirée: *I'll maim him tomorrow to make you do that...*

Sylvie felt an invigorating rage surge through her and she sprang to her feet. She went to the dressing chest and tidied her appearance. Not that she cared a jot for impressing Hugo with how she looked, but she would never let him see her as a sad little wreck. If he were guilty of this crime, he would revel in knowing how low he had brought her in perpetrating it. She pinched at her cheeks to revive colour in them and dabbed at her eyes to remove the stain of tears. With a final determined stare at her reflection she swished about and was soon heading for the stairs.

'I thought you might make an excuse not to see me.'

'It occurred to me to do so,' Sylvie retorted in a frigid tone. 'My sister is away from home, so you must call again if you wish to see her.'

'I know she is away from home. I have been loitering outside for some time, hoping she would go out without you.'

Sylvie immediately speared at him a suspicious look.

'Naturally, I wanted to see you alone. We have

secrets, you and I. I doubt you would want your sister knowing what they are,' he softly taunted her.

Hugo's tall frame was negligently propped on one elbow that lounged against the marble chimney-piece. He looked, Sylvie had to acknowledge, every inch the personable gentleman as he sauntered towards her. His clothes were fine, his blond hair shiny and those blue eyes so frankly direct. His appearance alone could fool a person into assuming he was an honourable fellow.

'Your sister has a fine house here. She did remarkably well in the marriage stakes.'

'I suspect you have more on your mind than my sister's good fortune,' Sylvie snapped.

'Indeed,' he drawled. 'I am here to remind you of yours.'

Sylvie whipped violent blue eyes to his face. 'My good fortune?'

'I have come to tell you that this week we will announce our betrothal and set an early date for our wedding.'

'You're quite mad to think I would ever consider you as a husband.' Her contempt was strong enough to make her voice shake.

Hugo's leisurely smile chilled Sylvie's blood for it hinted at an unshakeable confidence.

'*I* am quite mad to consider you for a wife. In

fact, if you do not curb that acid tongue of yours, I might change my mind and simply take you as my paramour and have done with it.'

Sylvie stared unwaveringly into steel-blue eyes brimming with callous satisfaction. Fiery needles of fear assaulted her skin—she sensed Hugo had not yet used his trump card.

'Ah, I see you are wondering how I know that's a role you're suited to.' His voice was speciously soothing as he came close to her, circled her, whilst a lustful gaze dropped insolently to her bodice. One of his fingers rose to touch the rim of lace that frothed over her small bosom.

Sylvie snatched herself away, simultaneously slapping out at his hand. A cruel grip stayed her fingers, twisted brutally when she would free herself.

'I would not do that, my love. I hold your future in my hand. I am your salvation, your only hope of a decent life.'

'A decent life?' Sylvie scoffed. '*With you?* You have no conception of what is *decent*. You are…' A hand spanned her mouth, squeezed slowly to cut off her disgust.

'Where do whores ply their trade? Do you know?' His voice was lulling, at odds with the vicious clutch he had on her chin. 'Haymarket, I would have said, perhaps the East End docks. I thought myself knowledgeable about the haunts of harlots.' He smiled into her wide, petrified eyes. 'I stand humbly corrected, for I learned recently, from a mutual friend of ours, that whores frequent the Great North Road. More particularly they use rooms in the George and Dragon Inn.'

Sylvie blinked and, as the full force of his knowledge made her gag against his restraint, she spontaneously bit into his flesh.

Hugo snatched away his stinging palm and it immediately became part of a fist that swung at her. It hovered, quivering, a few inches from her cheek as he checked, recalled where he was. His feral eyes held hers as he flexed his fingers, then licked away a bead of blood. 'I will very much enjoy making you regret that.' It was spoken in a voice of cool control. He might have been giving his opinion on the weather.

'You have scabs on your knuckles,' Sylvie accused hoarsely as she focused on the fingers that would have struck her. 'I know how you came by those. You have beaten John again, you foul bully. You have almost killed him.' Sylvie forced her eyes not to shirk from his. 'If you think that I will keep what I know to myself, you are very wrong. My sister and brother-in-law will soon be home and I shall waste no time in telling them everything…'

'You won't say anything to them or to anyone else,' he sneered over her words. He took a look at the crusty grazes. 'Those are nothing. I got the injury bare-knuckle sparring with a friend, and he'll tell you so.'

'You've bribed one of your cronies to lie for you,' Sylvie fumed.

'I take it Markham has brought news from Hertfordshire of Vance. I was hoping you would not yet know about your poor swain. Did Markham tell you that it was me who organised the search party? I did my duty as a concerned neighbour and set out to apprehend the culprit. There, don't be overwhelmed by my philanthropy, my dear. It was the least I could do.' He mocked the bright tears that had sprung to her eyes.

Swiftly Sylvie dashed a hand across her lashes. 'You started the rumour that undesirables had been spotted in the vicinity, didn't you?' she choked. 'You hoped to deflect suspicion from yourself. The only way you could make John tell of our elopement was to beat the secret from him.'

Hugo said nothing, simply cocked his head to one side while studying her. 'He is weak and cowardly. If he loved you he would endure any pain… die for you…before he betrayed you. What you see in such an imbecile is beyond me.'

'That I can believe! He is far beyond you in every way. He is kind and good…'

Hugo gestured irritation and swung away. 'Spare me, please, any bleeding heart histrionics. Your sentimental opinion of him no longer bothers me.' His voice had hardened with satisfaction. 'We have far more important matters to discuss: our wedding plans.'

'If I refuse to marry you?' Sylvie whispered. It was a pointless question; if he were prepared to batter John almost unto death, he would have no qualms about blackmailing her. She knew exactly what would be his answer: either she obeyed him or polite society would be treated to details of her aborted elopement. Her reputation would be irreparably sullied and her family would be shunned too, included in her disgrace.

Hugo chuckled as he watched her inner turmoil. 'I think you have an inkling of my intentions. I have not long been in town, but I hear on the grapevine that you are making quite an impression on a few *beau monde* bachelors. Mr Shepherd, Sir Alan Montague, even Guy Markham; all are rumoured to be scampering about your feet like loyal puppies. Will those gentleman still be so besotted, I wonder, when they discover that barely a month ago you were a farmer's doxy?'

His eyes lingered on her strained face and just for a moment Sylvie thought she noticed a glint of emotion hood his eyes. 'You should have carried on to Scotland and married him. I appreciated hearing that Vance hadn't acted the heartless philanderer and it was *you* who wanted to turn back. What changed your mind?' As the silence lengthened he shrugged. 'What matter? It suits me that you have left yourself uncommonly vulnerable, and of course I thanked Vance, too, for telling me so.'

Sylvie swallowed the nausea in her throat. Her own predicament was forgotten. Imagining the horror John must have endured before he betrayed her made her throat bob in anguish.

'You must make sure you show me proper gratitude for rescuing you from a sordid vocation as a fallen woman.'

Sylvie put up her chin and clashed her eyes on his.

'I am not a heartless beast.' The amusement in his tone proved he was not swayed by her bravado. 'I shall give you time to think it over. On Saturday, at two of the clock, I shall come to speak to you again. I hope, on that occasion, that your sister and brother-in-law are present too. I look forward to sharing our happy tidings with your kin.'

Chapter Thirteen

Sylvie shrank back into shadow as the coaches drew level.

A woman haughtily raised her lorgnette, peered determinedly, making Sylvie fear the old witch had somehow divined she was out to shamelessly visit an unsuspecting gentleman and beg his protection. Once the plush landau had passed, carrying away its inquisitive passenger, Sylvie again lifted a frayed corner of the blind obscuring the cab window. A shaft of sunlight warmed her peeking countenance.

Minutes before she had given the driver instructions to convey her to Upper Brook Street before collapsing, breathless, into the creaky squabs of the hackney. Now with her senses steadying, it occurred to her to question why she should have instinctively chosen to flee to a gentleman of limited acquaintance rather than wait and pour her heart out to her sister when she arrived home. In her frenzied dash to ready herself to leave the house, and find transport, it had not entered her mind, either, that the Marquess might not want to become embroiled in her problems.

The thought plagued her now. Their truce was still quite fragile and of short duration. They had been at loggerheads far longer than they had been friends. Adam had flirted with her yesterday, and looked sympathetic when Guy delivered his awful news about John's injuries. But Hugo was his godfather's son. He might remind her of his loyalties, and that confronting Hugo was her family's duty, not his. He might add that she had three brothers-in-law to safeguard her should she want to spare her father the exertion.

Her worries were valid but she would *not*, she impressed upon herself, believe that the man to whom she had naturally turned for protection would let her down. Adam had already earned her trust by keeping a secret. Despite their bickering, he had shown her loyalty and respect. Once he knew how vilely Hugo Robinson had treated her he would somehow make it all come right, she was sure he would. It was not so long ago he had liked her well enough to propose marriage. But for her regrettable immaturity he might have been her closest kin…her husband…

A frustrated sigh escaped as something occurred to her. What if Adam were *not* at home? He probably would be out, she realised with an odd mix of disappointment and relief. It was a clement afternoon in spring and few fashionable people would be found moping indoors in such glorious weather.

She sneaked another glance at carriages and pedestrians ambling along the Strand. Her lively eyes darted here and there, then chanced upon a sleek vehicle weaving niftily between lumbering carts. It was a low-sprung curricle and in harness were coal-black horses…

For no more than a second Sylvie gazed upon her quarry—and his elegant companion, unidentifiable beneath a wide-brimmed bonnet—before she rapped urgently to give the jarvey new instructions.

'Eh?' the man bellowed back, the snarl in his voice letting Sylvie clearly know that he was neither pleased nor fully cognisant with her plan to abort the journey to Upper Brook Street.

'Which rig d'ya mean?' he demanded, jerking on the reins to slow his nags, thereby making the contraption shudder.

'The curricle and fine black horses… There!'
Sylvie indicated with a finger stabbing the air. She
hung a little further out of the cab window and
again pointed at the vehicle hurtling away in the
opposite direction, a wiry tiger intrepidly clinging
to its rear. 'Could you not just turn about and follow them?'

'Oh yes…yes…'course I can,' the jarvey muttered sarcastically. 'Nuffin', is it, to turn me cab
about wiv 'awses 'n coaches 'n all sorts o' daw-
dlers in me parf.'

'Will an extra shilling on the fare help to ease
the inconvenience?' Sylvie swayed her swanlike
neck to coax him with a bright, enquiring smile.

The jarvey glowered at her over a slumped
shoulder. 'Risk me life an' limbs, not to mention
me nags, for a poxy shillin'? Make it an 'alf a
crown, then.' He accepted the bribe with bad grace.

Sylvie quickly cast back her memory to calcu-
late the value of the coins in her reticule, then nodded. 'It's the curricle, up ahead, with…'

'I know…wiv black 'awses,' he finished for her
in a martyred tone.

It seemed, once the sulky driver had got the
outfit pointing in the right direction, he entered
into the spirit of the chase. The hackney pelted
along the Strand in pursuit of Adam's curricle.

Sylvie braced a hand either side of her as she bounced on the seat and tried to close her ears to the abuse that accompanied their lethal progress. Without daring to take a peek outside to see, she knew pedestrians and vehicles were scattering out of their way. They took a sharp turn that jolted her into a corner, then, on finding her balance, and her regrets at ever having set in motion this lunatic, the vehicle ground to a halt.

'Woman in 'ere wants you, guvnor.'

The bald statement startled a frown from Sylvie, but it was a moment or two more before she fully understood and cringed. Gingerly she lifted the leather an inch. A handsome, angular visage tilted to the right as though to see beneath it. No doubt Adam was keen to discover which hussy had the audacity to importune him in broad daylight. Sylvie dropped the blind to prevent him succeeding, and sank into the cushions. From the glimpse she had had of his expression, she could tell he was not in the least flattered to know he had been stalked.

Although she had only snatched a momentary glance at the imposing townhouse outside which they had stopped, and the comely woman alighting from the curricle, she recognised them both. Recently she had entered the premises as a welcomed guest and been taught the finer points of gin rummy by the Marquess of Rockingham. Sylvie doubted that Lady Burdett would again invite her to a card evening should her jaunt today ever be uncovered. The dowager countess had looked exceedingly displeased to have her escort so rudely whipped away by another woman.

Sylvie heard a door abruptly slam. A tuneless whistling was the jarvey's nod to nonchalance as footsteps approached. The cab door was opened, just a little way, as though to shield its passenger from view.

Sylvie stilled her nervous hands by folding them neatly on her lap. Her stomach's writhing was less easily calmed as she gazed into dark, saturnine features. 'I…I wanted to see you urgently.'

'So I gather,' Adam replied in an odd tone that left Sylvie unsure whether amusement or reproof was dominant.

'I…we have been chasing you along the street,' Sylvie blurted, then, belatedly appreciated the silence.

Adam got in. 'I take it at some point I shall know why.' It was a mere suggestion as he sat and closed the door.

''Ere…where to?' the jarvey demanded huffily. ''Alf a crown don't cover sittin' in me cab wiv a gent, nor nuthin' else, mind…'

'Grove House, St James's,' Adam instructed the jarvey without once looking away from Sylvie's blushing face. As the cab pulled away, he instructed his tiger to wait with the curricle until he returned.

Still suffering from hearing the jarvey's embarrassing ruling, Sylvie stuttered, 'I…I'm sorry if I have interrupted your meeting with Lady Burdett. She seemed a little…put out. Was she expecting you to accompany her indoors?'

Adam shrugged. 'Possibly, but I would have had to disappoint her. I had other plans for this afternoon and simply brought her home when one of her cattle went lame in Bond Street.' The truthful explanation caused him a wry, private grimace for how very odd a coincidence it had been. The moment he had slowed to politely acknowledge his erstwhile mistress, she had instructed her driver to check the health of the greys. Lo and behold, the fellow had noticed that one of the leads had an injury. Adam had had a mind to take a look too, but, with little else to do other than meet Guy for an afternoon of gaming, he had decided to allow her little manoeuvre.

Nevertheless, he was becoming irritated with Deborah for refusing to accept that her role as his paramour was over. He was also irritated because the reason he no longer wanted *her* was… His eyes settled on a pale oval face that was veiled by a bonnet brim and shaded daylight. He quirked a smile and Sylvie responded instantly, her full lips sweetly curving to display pearly teeth.

He felt a responsive tightening in his gut spread to his loins and he mocked himself for the way she could so easily disarm him. She had shown concern for Jake's predicament and touched his heart, but she wasn't a sweet innocent, he impressed on himself. She had a lover; she also had ambition and it was the unanticipated venal side to her character that left a bitter taste in his mouth. She might be in town seeking a mate, she might even have hinted that she would like it to be him, but she cherished her farmer. Yesterday he had witnessed raw proof of that when she learned of John Vance's injuries. Her distress had been heartbreaking to observe.

Adam had wanted to hold her, ease her pain, yet hateful feelings gnawed at him too because another man had her heart and soul. As though to deny he was still in the throes of such an invidious emotion, he said quietly, 'I did not have a chance yesterday to tell you that I am very sorry about John Vance. The news must have come as a terrible shock.'

A nod was all the answer he received.

'I hope he will make a full and speedy recovery. I'm sure he will,' he softly soothed as he noticed the dew he had brought to her eyes by mentioning any of it.

Sylvie quickly nodded again, showing appreciation of his concern. It was a prime opportunity to now say she was sure she knew which villain had perpetrated such a cowardly attack…and why. Still she felt nervous of describing intimate details of her abuse, yet she must if she were to bring accusations against Hugo. She knew Hugo would defend himself in the way he had threatened: by saying she had teased and encouraged him.

'I did not mean to embarrass you in public just now. I know I ought not have acted so wild and impulsive, but I'm afraid, rightly or wrongly, that seems to be my way.' A peek from beneath twin fans of dusky lashes told her that an oblique apology had done little to alter his demeanour.

'Your way…to do what?'

She hesitated, and then an idea, inspired and persistent, took her concentration. If he would fall in with such a plan it might solve everything. Hugo was a coward; he would never cross the Marquess of Rockingham, or insult such a powerful gentleman's wife. John Vance would be a good friend of Lady Rockingham's. He would be safe! 'It is my way…to boldly remind you of something you said yesterday,' Sylvie whispered.

Adam frowned. 'Did I say something that upset you?'

'No…not at all. You asked me…if I was proposing marriage to you.'

'And were you?' he asked huskily.

'Yes, I was.'

Adam lounged back against the squabs, the expression in his eyes concealed behind languid lids. 'Well, I am naturally honoured and flattered, but—'

'Don't laugh at me!' Sylvie choked. She put up her chin and gazed at him with proud entreaty glossing her eyes. 'Say you will marry me, please. You wanted me once. I have not changed that much…' She hesitated, wondering if such an observation was wise. 'Well, I have changed quite a lot, actually. But for the good,' she stressed. 'Even my mother says that I have improved. I will be a good wife.'

'I'm sure you will,' Adam said hoarsely, sitting forward to rest his elbows on his knees. 'But not to me.'

'Why not?' she demanded rather indignantly.

Long, patrician fingers cradled his face; a bark of laughter emerged through them. 'You said you had improved. That is the sort of blunt question I might have expected fired at me two years ago from that saucy urchin.'

'But I *am* still her,' Sylvie insisted and slid forward on the seat to grab one of his hands in emphasis. She pulled it away from his dark features and unconsciously lavished attention on it.

Adam watched the soft, slender fingers that were coaxing him with little strokes.

'I know you liked her…that silly girl. It wasn't just chivalry to protect her reputation. You *wanted* to marry me when I was a saucy urchin.' Sylvie's coquettish little smile teased him.

'How did you know I wanted to marry you?'

Blue and brown eyes merged, tangled before Sylvie looked away.

'Come, you told me once before how you knew I hadn't proposed out of duty. You were right. Tell me again now.'

Sylvie's touch on his skin stilled and her fingertips withdrew an inch or so before they were captured, held fast.

'Why won't you tell me? Are you afraid it might end as it did before? With something you don't like?'

'No, of course not,' Sylvie murmured, but her eyes avoided his.

'If ever I marry, I should want a wife, Sylvie, who does not cringe when I kiss her.'

'I won't…' was breathlessly shot back at him.

'You did,' he countered.

'I didn't mean to…'

'But you did.'

'I'm sorry. I won't do it again,' Sylvie said and raised wide appealing eyes to his. 'I promise I won't do it again,' she stressed in a staunch, trembling voice.

'That's very brave of you,' Adam said quietly. 'But quite unnecessary.'

Sylvie gazed appealingly at him. 'Surely you won't turn me down because of *that*. I'll do what you want…anything…I swear I'll be a proper wife…'

With a curse Adam flung away her hands and slung himself into a corner of the coach. Sylvie slid awkwardly in the opposite direction.

'Quite the little martyr, aren't you?' he mocked with dulcet savagery. 'You'll marry me, tolerate me in your bed, and when I'm done, no doubt you'll dream of your farmer.'

Sylvie's wide eyes slew from a sightless contemplation of the window to the rigid planes of his face. He sounded enraged.

'No…it's not like that…' she quavered. 'John and me…we…it is not what you think!' she resorted to uttering tearfully.

'You love him, don't you?'

'Yes…but…'

'Why don't you just wait a while?' he snarled over her further attempt to explain her fondness for her friend. 'Vance will recover in time, and my advice to you is marry him as soon as he is able to walk down the aisle. Marry him, Sylvie, or, by God, I'll let it be known that you're a mercenary little trollop who was seduced by ambition and money into jilting the man you love. Do it! I have no more stomach for keeping your secrets.' He suddenly yanked back the blind, flooding the carriage with harsh light, and stared out. 'You're practically home,' he gritted. 'Forgive me for not seeing you to your door.'

With a shout for the cab to halt, he was soon out on the pavement. A handful of coins hit the battered hide where recently he had lounged. 'Pay the man the going rate for using his cab.'

June sighed, stabbed her needle into her embroidery, then pushed away the frame. 'Shall I go up to Sylvie's room and see if I can persuade her to come down for dinner?'

'I think you ought leave her be,' her husband responded, closing the book on his lap. William picked up his whisky and sipped. 'It is a horrible thing that has happened to her friend. You know how close they were. You must give her some time to quietly mull it over.'

'But I'm…I'm not sure it is just worry over John Vance that is making her so miserable,' June interrupted, looking reflective. 'When I arrived home from Lady Forster's this afternoon Sylvie was out. Molly said she had had a visitor. Hugo Robinson came to call.'

'I didn't think your sister liked Robinson.' William looked perplexed. 'He must have admirably persuasive powers if she agreed to go out with him, without a chaperon. When last I saw them together in Hertfordshire, the atmosphere seemed positively frosty.'

June shook her head. 'They did not go out together. Molly said that the gentleman left before Sylvie did. By all accounts he was not here for long. I expect Sylvie sent him off with a flea in his ear. When Sylvie returned she simply said she had been out for some fresh air. It could not have done her much good, for she looked very subdued, as though she had been crying. She has been in her room ever since.'

The object of anxiety suddenly curtailed further discussion between husband and wife by appearing in the sitting room. June immediately went to fondly embrace her sister. 'I was just saying to William how peaky you looked earlier today.'

'I was tired,' Sylvie said with a slight smile. 'I feel a mite better now.'

'That's good! Perhaps getting out of the house for a while was the cure, after all.' June patted one of Sylvie's hands in emphasis. She drew her to a chair, informing her, 'I received a letter from Mama today. She hopes we are all well. She also hopes that some local news will not reach as far as London. She asks me to be alert and, if I can, to shield you from it.'

'She is referring to what has happened to John,' Sylvie said on a vague frown. 'Perhaps she thinks such awful news will make me rescind my promise to find a husband.'

'She seeks to protect you from hurt, Sylvie, that is all. She knows how close are you and John. I expect she is fretting on your tender feelings. Mama is not to know we already have the woeful tale from Guy Markham.'

Sylvie nodded, twisted a small smile of acceptance of that.

'I do not mind if you read the letter.' June glanced at her husband. William was flicking over pages of his book and maintaining a tactful silence whilst his wife dealt with family politics.

Sylvie shook her head, declining the offer. 'Does Mama say how John is?'

'He was still unconscious at the time of her writing. I expect a deep sleep is necessary in healing a bad head injury.' June hoped her layman's opinion was sound. 'By now, of course, he might be improved.'

Sylvie agreed quietly, 'Yes, we must hope and pray he is improved.' After a brief silence she took in a deep breath and enquired, 'Are we to go out tonight?'

June stole a look at William. 'Not if you do not want to. We could stay home and play cards, or chess. You like a game of chess, Sylvie.'

'It might be nice to go out,' Sylvie suggested and endorsed that with a smile.

'Well, if you would like to, we could join Guy and his friends and go to Vauxhall.' June's bright expression indicated she hoped the suggestion would be approved. Nevertheless, she considerately added, 'Or if you prefer a quieter entertainment, there is the Beethoven recital…'

'Vauxhall is fine,' Sylvie interrupted quickly. 'Actually, I should very much like to see Guy.'

Chapter Fourteen

'Have you received any news from home about John Vance?' Sylvie's tone combined optimism and apprehension as she awaited her escort's reply.

Guy's jaunty demeanour had deflated on hearing the hesitant question and he frowned at the ground. They continued their promenade in the pleasure gardens beneath globe lamps jigging in windy trees. Finally Guy sighed deeply. 'Wasn't going to mention it again, Miss Sylvie, even though it is better news than last I gave you.' He tipped his nut-brown head, indicating a stocky fellow some yards away. The jovial-looking man was with some friends close to the orchestra podium. 'Pomeroy's just back from visiting Janet. He reports that your friend has woken up. That's good. No further forward with catching the accursed vil-

lain who did it to him. That's bad.' Guy's fierce
glower foundered as he noticed that Sylvie was
anxiously attending to his every word. 'Wish I had
not mentioned the first thing about it,' he admitted
meekly. 'Hate to think I was the one who brought
bad tidings. Made you so sad.'

'But you have now given me far better news,'
Sylvie said sweetly. 'Made me glad. For that I
thank you very much.' Sylvie looked searchingly
at Guy. 'Has John managed to give any clues as to
who attacked him?'

'By all accounts the poor chap don't remember
much. Perhaps he will, given time. Great healer,
you know… time.'

Sylvie cast down her face, deep in thought. Had
John really no memory of being attacked? Or had
he been cowed into silence by Hugo's threats of re-
prisal should he expose him as a vicious thug and
a liar? Was John in adequate possession of his fac-
ulties and still trying to protect her by keeping secret his assailant's identity? The only way to know
for sure was to return to Hertfordshire and to beg
to be allowed to see him. A heavy exhalation escaped her as she wondered whether John's parents
would let her near him.

'I *have* made you sad again.' Guy gave a morose
shake of the head on hearing her melancholy sigh.

Sylvie immediately took his arm. Just as she began to endorse that comfort with a verbal reassurance, her words were drowned out by a couple of raucous revellers capering, with dangerously unsteady gait, along the path towards them.

People of all social classes came to enjoy Vauxhall Pleasure Gardens. Rich aristocrats with their elegant ladies rubbed shoulders with humble clerks squiring stout wives got up in Sunday finery. A waterfall's soothing melody was just audible amid the noise, then the opening bars of a waltz tempered the cacophony.

Guy slowed his pace to observe the hectic activity all around. He raised an eyebrow at Sylvie. 'Nice to see people having fun…' was his philanthropic observation.

Sylvie gave him a smile. John was awake! It was enough reason to be cheerful, she impressed upon herself. There was no guilt surely in celebrating his improvement. With that in mind, she again slipped her hand through Guy's arm and urged him on. She was becoming quite fond of Guy, she realised wistfully. He was a kind gentleman who, she estimated, would be a staunchly loyal spouse. But Guy had not repeated his impulsive proposal and she baulked at embarrassing them both by reminding him of it. Besides, Hugo Robinson would carry out his threat to parade her shame in the face of any potential suitor, and she would hate Guy to be pilloried for his decency. As they strolled in companionable quiet, Sylvie wondered how Guy would react should he discover how precarious was her virtuous reputation. He would not shun her, she was sure; in fact, he might adopt the role of knight errant and offer her his services.

She bravely conquered the inclination to propose to Guy there and then and secure her protector. She had a while yet to find a solution to her predicament. If none presented itself before the appointed hour, then she must tell June and William of the torments inflicted on John and her by Hugo, and make them faithfully promise to deal with it in a way least likely to harm their parents. The swine had promised to allow her until Saturday to ponder on his proposal and she believed he would at least honour that.

She drew in an inspiriting breath as her mind returned to dwelling on the humiliation she had suffered from a different quarter mere hours ago. With childlike trust she had put all her hope for salvation in a man she had believed to be her hero. For him she had swallowed her pride, humbled herself. With stark brutality he had shown his true character and mocked her—insulted her. She felt a fool for having harboured an instinct that she was special to him. Now she knew exactly what the Marquess of Rockingham thought of her. And now she knew what she thought of him.

Hateful man! Sylvie inwardly fumed, yet she was equally angry with herself. Naïvely she had believed that, despite their differences and their squabbles, he would rescue her from Hugo's malevolence. And while she had sat alone with him in the coach, risking her reputation once more, and struggling with vital decisions, what had been *his* abiding concern?

A kiss! Sylvie felt a scornful laugh clog her throat. He was ruled by lust and she had no business being surprised on knowing it. Time and again she had heard the rumours about the notorious Rockinghams. *Rakes and rogues, one and all,* she had once heard her aunt Phyllis Chamberlain describe a clan that was rumoured to have in its ancestry Mohocks, corsairs and members of the Hell Fire Club. Her aunt was wont to exaggerate. Sylvie doubted she had on that occasion.

Nevertheless, Sylvie wished she had known kissing could be quite nice... A wry inner smile acknowledged that, with hindsight, it had been rather wonderful, nothing like that time when Hugo had slobbered on her, making her feel sick. Since the day Adam had held her in his arms and kissed her, she had hoped he might do it again. Perhaps, if things had gone well between them this afternoon, she might have had a chance to tell him so…

Now, of course, she would rather kiss a frog! Besides, she knew he could only do it well because of excessive practice.

The image she now had in her mind, of his hard mouth moulded to another woman's lips, made a knot tighten in her stomach. Sylvie tipped up her head and stared through splintery vision at lights starring in foliage. Why should she care about that? He was beastly and she hated him!

'Shall we make our way towards the orchestra podium?' June had approached on William's arm whilst Sylvie was attempting to quell her turbulent thoughts. 'Or perhaps you would sooner join Lady Forster's party? We have an invitation to join her in her supper box.'

Sylvie blinked away the moisture in her eyes. 'I don't mind if we do.' Her sister was treated to a scintillating smile.

'Oh, Adam is here,' June informed her as she stretched her petite frame up on to tiptoe to see over a multitude of heads. 'Shall we first go over and say hello?' Assuming her sister's answer would be in the affirmative, June headed off in that direction.

Guy made to follow, but was halted after a pace or two by a gentle tug on his arm. 'Do you mind if we stroll on a little way?' It was a bright, persuasive suggestion. 'It is a long while since I visited Vauxhall. I'd like to see the grottoes and pavilions.'

Guy looked surprised that they were to ignore the arrival of one of the *ton's* most illustrious personages. However, he nodded indulgently at Sylvie. 'Speak to him later on then, shall we?' He bent his head to whisper conspiratorially, 'Doubt he'll miss us. Looks quite cosy with Lady Burdett…'

Sylvie sent a subtle look slanting back over her shoulder. Deborah Burdett did, indeed, appear to have a possessive clutch on his arm, with her face positioned close to his. With sudden insight she realised she had been hopelessly naïve over that too. Of course, the young widow was his mistress.

'She is his *chère amie*,' Sylvie said, mostly to herself.

'One of their number…' Guy chortled, then looked stricken. He blushed and a finger fiddled at his throat, ruining the effect of his intricately styled cravat. 'Didn't mean to be indiscreet or indelicate,' he muttered nervously. 'Don't tell your papa you heard that from me. Have my hide, he will.'

Sylvie gave him a soulful ghost of a smile.

'We're friends, Guy. I would never get you into trouble over such a paltry thing. Of course I already knew. Everybody knows about the Marquess and his women…don't they?'

'S'pose they do,' Guy agreed with a strengthening confidence. Suddenly he clamped her fingers on his sleeve with a large hand and veered away at speed, making Sylvie trot to keep up with him. He abruptly halted in a secluded, unlit pathway and craned his neck about the screening hedge. 'Damme! Just noticed that Robinson fellow coming our way. Hope he didn't see us. Can do without *his* tedious company. Mind you, credit where it's due: he did play a part in trying to search out the cur who attacked your friend Vance.'

Guy continued bobbing his head this way and that to peer cautiously about the privet.

'What are you up to, Markham? Do you owe someone money?'

The sardonic drawl emerged from the shadows and made both Guy and Sylvie swing about. Adam had materialised behind them and was lounging into the hedge, hands thrust negligently into his pockets.

'Shh…' Guy slapped a finger to his lips. 'That fellow Robinson is just the other side of this bush,' he mouthed. 'Can't abide the man even if he is Sir

Anthony's son.' Suddenly Guy ducked his lofty frame and cursed beneath his breath. 'Think he's spotted me.'

Sylvie felt ice stalk her spine. 'I'd much rather avoid him,' she hastily whispered. The idea that Hugo might discover her lurking in the dark, with two gentlemen unrelated to her, sent her into a retreat. He was deluded to think of her as his intended and was mad enough to seek to slander her for any supposed slight. Adam knew of her disastrous elopement, but not of the other awful things that bound John and her to Hugo in a conspiracy of silence. Oddly she felt it was imperative that only she be allowed to tell him of it. As for Guy, she hoped he would never be privy to her tangled web of shame.

'You stay with the Marquess, I'll head him off,' Guy hissed. Following the striking of a heroic pose, he plunged away in a snap of foliage.

Acutely aware of the ensuing silence, and that this afternoon's hostility was still a potent force between them, Sylvie peeped through the opening, preparing to leave when the coast was clear.

'Have you hooked him? Perhaps Robinson turned up at an inopportune moment and spoiled it for you.'

'I beg your pardon?' Sylvie swished about in a

rustle of pastel silk to show Adam a beautifully haughty countenance.

'I would lay money that you intended luring Markham somewhere secluded to remind him of his proposal. As I declined to marry you, I take it he's your second choice.'

Immediate humiliation sent a surge of blood to heat Sylvie's cheeks. 'Well, you would lose your stake,' she exploded. 'Not least because I would far sooner be his wife than yours!' A sudden, awful thought occurred to her. 'Did you follow us here so you could warn him against me?' Her outrage nearly strangled the words in her throat; it also rendered her deaf to his curt, negative response. 'How dare you!' she fumed, stalking closer to him, her blonde head thrown back and violet eyes sparking dangerously. She stepped within striking distance, her small fingers clenched at her sides. 'You asked me once if I understood who you were. Let me tell you, I certainly do now! You are the most appallingly arrogant man I have ever had the misfortune to—'

The remainder of her censure was smothered as she was hauled against a lean muscular body and a warm silky mouth slid to occupy her parted lips.

Sylvie reflexively struggled, and a small hand arced up to slap at his face.

He ducked nimbly out of harm's way and a travesty of a laugh scratched his throat. 'Just checking whether you were being sincere this afternoon. I seem to recall being offered certain favours. In fact, *anything I want* springs to mind.'

'That was before I fully understood how shallow you are.' Sylvie gulped in a breath, trying to steady her pounding heart. 'I humbled myself to chase after you and propose and what was your abiding concern in it all? A kiss!' she said scornfully.

'There's a lot more to it than a kiss, Sylvie, and you know it,' Adam said softly. 'Don't pretend to be the innocent with me. I keep your secrets…or have you conveniently forgotten that I know you and Vance bedded down together at the George and Dragon?'

'You don't know anything,' Sylvie whispered fiercely. 'You simply measure every man by your own lax standards. Why don't you go and find Lady Burdett? I know she appreciates your company more than I do.' Sylvie flung herself about and, with a cursory glance through the hedge to check Hugo was gone, she sought to urgently escape the other man bent on tormenting her.

'What are you doing?'

The indolent query was coupled with a grip on her wrist that brought her again into dark vegetation.

Sylvie vainly attempted to fling off those firm fingers. 'I am going to find my sister and brother-in-law.' The announcement was icily concise.

'Alone? Are you aware that only a certain class of woman would walk in Vauxhall unescorted?'

'Of course!' Sylvie's tone was sweetly sour. 'And, as you told me this afternoon that I am a trollop, I am surprised you bother mentioning it.'

She realised he was curbing his temper from the rigid set to his jaw and the way his lashes abruptly veiled his eyes. Nevertheless she tilted her chin and renewed her effort to free herself.

'Don't try my patience, Sylvie.' It was a mild request.

'Why ever not? You constantly test mine.' She glared at him over a shoulder. 'You are doing so now. Unless you are offering to immediately escort me back to my family, please remove your hand from my person.'

'I can't.'

'Why ever not?' she asked again.

'Because if I do that, you'll run away before I have a chance to talk to you.'

'I think that today, sir, you have said more than enough to me already.'

'Ah, there we have the problem,' he countered.

'For I can't decide whether I said too much or not enough.'

'Let me solve your dilemma. I have no intention of listening to any more of your threats or insults.' Sylvie's eyes were brimful of pride and unshed tears as she challenged him. 'If you wish to betray the trust I had in you…then do so. It will not surprise me—I am no longer that silly girl who believed Adam Townsend was her friend. Do your worst! I don't care.' After a combatant moment in which their eyes strained, she turned her head.

'I'm sorry.'

Sylvie slowly faced him. 'For what are you sorry? Calling me a trollop? Accusing me of scheming to trap Guy? Kissing me in anger just now as though it was a punishment?'

'It wasn't…it was desperation. Never mind,' he muttered, noting her bewilderment. 'I'm sorry for all of it,' he stated softly.

Sylvie searched his earth-dark eyes for a sign of mockery, but he returned her gaze with almost humble directness. She took a conciliatory step closer to him. 'Then why…?'

Adam mirrored the move in equal part so less than a few inches separated them. 'I'm jealous, my dear, that's all.' A self-deprecatory grimace twisted his mouth. A finger was raised, slowly, to brush with infinite gentleness against alabaster skin draped with spiralling silver curls. 'No, it's not all. I'm angry because I know you love someone else, yet are prepared to settle for me. And I'm frustrated. I know most marriages are commercial ventures, so I've no need to pine for you to love me like a sentimental fool… yet still I do. And I'm obsessed with wanting to know why you and Vance ran off, but—'

'So he would leave us alone.' The words erupted in a trembling sigh. Their eyes clung together until the sense of relief that brave utterance had given her propelled her into continuing the confession while frowning into dusky shadows. 'We thought if we were man and wife he would not dare again hurt either of us by word or deed. But then, at the George and Dragon, you were there and it seemed…wrong to go on. John wanted to carry on to Gretna; perhaps if we had, he would still be well. It's my fault that he has been hurt so badly.' The guilt and grief she had subdued suddenly rose up to wedge in her throat, blocking her voice. She covered her face with trembling hands and sobbed.

For a stunned moment Adam looked down at her bowed bright head. Tentatively, as though be-wildered, he reached out to enfold her quaking form. As soon as her avid arms wound about his waist she was anchored there, his body curving about hers as though to absorb her shuddering. His hands soothed in long strong strokes at her back before curving over her scalp and turning her face up to his.

'You *know* who attacked John Vance?' His voice was so hoarse the question was virtually inaudible.

Sylvie nodded and smeared the wet from her face. 'He has done it before. He hates John simply because I cherish him. He hates me too and only wants to marry me so he can hurt me again and again…'

'*Hugo Robinson?*' The name emerged in a voice of husky astonishment.

Sylvie nodded her face against his chest. 'He came to see me at Grove House today. He had beaten John into betraying our secret. He knows of our elopement. He threatens that if I do not marry him very soon he will spread gossip about that scandal and…and other shameful things too,' she finished in a voice that was a mere thread of sound.

Adam cradled her head against his shoulder and she leaned into the comfort, uninhibitedly cuddling him back while fresh sobs racked her body.

'What shameful things, Sylvie?' A soothing stroking at her face, at her hair, lulled her until she allowed her degradation to steal into her mind. A hand hovered at her face as she viewed mental images filtered through her fingers.

'He said if I met him alone in the wood, he wouldn't bully John any more. He said he would leave us be. But when I got there…when I got there…he wouldn't talk of that at all. He talked of lewd things and what I must do to please him. When I tried to leave he wouldn't let me. He tore my clothes and pushed me to the ground then…fell on me, biting and touching…' She swallowed violently and repeatedly as she felt the nausea rise in her throat. 'He tried to hold me down, but I scratched and kicked and… and when he let go of my hands to unbutton his breeches, there was a stone close by my fingers and I hit him. It knocked him off me. He swore, called me a wanton who'd teased him. He shouted out that terrible things would happen to us both, but I kept running…' Fresh tears suddenly racked her slender frame and she gripped hard at Adam as though she would fuse their bodies. 'It's my fault he has nearly killed John.'

Adam's lashes dropped, trapping the spiteful heat in his eyes. He bent his dark head until a cheek rested against a silky crown of hair. Through a throat that had virtually closed in anguish he vowed, 'No, it's not your fault, Sylvie. You must believe me, I swear it is not your fault.'

Sylvie gulped in a breath, slowly becoming conscious of the quiet. Awkwardly she moved to straighten herself so his support was barely needed. 'Apart from John, I have never told anyone that. If my papa knew…but he cannot…he is not well, you see. And my mama would die from knowing…so how could I…? William would call him out, of course, then the whole world would know… So, it's best to say nothing. But…I don't know what to do.' The wretched admission was coupled with a hysterical giggle. Belatedly she tried to stifle the sound with a hand that then sprang upwards to stop the tears before they flowed. With a calming little sniff she decided to neaten her dishevelled appearance. Her dress and hair were pulled and patted.

Adam watched her fanatically through eyes that glittered like stars.

'I don't know what to do.' Her despair emerged this time as a level statement.

'It doesn't matter, sweetheart.' Adam finally found a voice gruff with tenderness. 'I do.'

Chapter Fifteen

'You will apologise for that remark, sirrah!'

Sir Anthony Robinson leaned heavily on his walking stick and took a few laboured steps to confront his son.

Beneath an outward show of petulance lurked calculation as Hugo slid a crafty look at his sire. The ulcer on his leg was not healing; in fact, he could see the poison was stretching the cloth of his breeches. He could afford to curb his impatience a little longer. His father was a man approaching his seventy-second year, and he was ailing.

Hugo's callous desire for his father's demise had festered over many years from resentment, for Sir Anthony had taken his baronetcy at just eighteen. Hugo was half a decade older than that and deemed it high time *he* was handed the reins. As he watched his father wince and shift position, it encouraged him to bide his time. With luck he might soon inherit his birthright. Thereafter he would never again need to stoop to importune for a few extra pounds to eke out his allowance. Once Rivendale was his, there would be some changes made, he promised himself as a scornful eye ran over furniture of simple elegance.

A penitent expression accompanied Hugo's apology. 'I'm sorry, Father. I didn't mean to sound ungrateful. I know you are generous. But I'm living in town now and things are more expensive for me than in the country. I have my own lodgings in Fenner Street and bills to pay. Plus there are some additional expenses I have to meet.'

'I take it you're referring to the cost of your drinking and fornication, for why else would you put up in such a rookery?'

Humiliation mottled Hugo's complexion, yet he curbed his temper. Sir Anthony was a man of impeccable manners. Clearly he was furious to so coarsely shout at his son, especially as Lady Robinson was at her embroidery in the next room. Hugo was beginning to fear that on this occasion some extra blunt might not easily be extracted from his father.

He bowed his blond head, looking suitably chastened. 'I admit that I have vices. What young man hasn't?' He appealed to Sir Anthony's world-liness. When his conspiratorial wink elicited no more than a shake of an iron-grey head, he added with boyish charm, 'I won over fifty guineas at Newmarket recently.'

Sir Anthony waved aside the excuse. 'And lost double the sum on the next nag, I don't doubt.' But he was a little mollified by his son's humbler de-meanour. He searched in a pocket and withdrew a bank note of low denomination. 'That's all you will get from me until your money is due. Don't think to return in a day or two with more tales of woe.'

Hugo swiftly slipped the money into a pocket. 'Thank you, Father.' His gratitude was an after-thought, sent over a shoulder, just before he closed the door to the library. In the hallway he spotted his mother purposefully hovering. As she spied her only child, Susannah Robinson immediately approached to talk to him.

With a perfunctory dip of his head Hugo mut-tered, 'Ma'am', by way of greeting, before strid-ing on.

'Are you leaving so soon?'

When he nodded without turning around, Su-sannah started after him. Catching up with him, she took her son's arm. 'Why don't you stay to dine and leave in the morning? It is a long way—'

'I have to go, Mother,' Hugo interjected a trifle impatiently, disengaging his elbow from her fond clutch. 'Business to attend to, you know.'

Susannah watched the tall figure striding from the house, then turned to glumly retrace her steps and find her husband.

She arrived in the library just as Sir Anthony was in the process of dropping his quite considerable girth into a chair. He sighed and, releasing his grip, let the cane clatter where it would. His wife dutifully picked up the stick and rested it against the wall within his reach.

She stepped back and forth across the rug, darting glances at her fatigued spouse. 'Did Hugo come to see how we fare?'

A mirthless laugh preceded Sir Anthony's reply. 'No; he came on his own account. He is run through his money already.'

'London is an expensive place to be during the Season,' his wife ventured.

'It is not the cost of things, Susannah. His allowance is ample. Most young men could live like princes on what I give him. It is not even as if he had spent the cash on a lease to a fine address. He is living in a hovel. He is become a drunk and a wastrel and well you know it.'

Susannah sat down in a wingchair opposite her

husband and picked distractedly at threads on the arm before she spoke. 'Sometimes I wonder: where is my old Hugo? As a child he was not overly affectionate, but since he returned from his Grand Tour he seems to have no time for us at all.'

'He finds time enough when he wants something.' Sir Anthony's succinct observation drew a sigh from his wife, and a sad little gesture.

'I'm sure marriage will mellow him. I have a feeling he has only gone to London because Silver Meredith is there. Perhaps he is spending too much—acting lavish—in an effort to impress her. She is an uncommonly pretty girl and is bound to attract much attention. But Gloria likes Hugo and would sanction the match.'

'Well, don't get your hopes up. As I understand it, Silver Meredith holds no high opinion of my heir at all,' Sir Anthony stated bluntly, but refrained from destroying his wife's romantic view of their son's impecuniosity. 'And from what I have seen and heard of his conduct lately, I cannot blame her for that!'

Susannah bridled at her husband's sharp criticism of their solitary offspring. 'There are other nice young ladies hereabouts who would be honoured to have him pay a call. He ought to come home and—'

'No, he ought not come home,' Sir Anthony quietly disagreed. 'In fact, had he not chosen to move to town, I would have suggested he do so. I am starting to hear rumours about him I don't like, Susannah; tales of womanising and drunkenness and rowdy behaviour in the local villages.'

Susannah was stricken as much by the worrying news as by her husband's gravity. Strongly she defended her son, but her voice was trembling. 'He is a red-blooded young man, Tony. We must expect he will act a little…wild. He will change when he has a wife and family, I'm sure.'

'I'd like to hope you are right, my dear, I really would,' was all Sir Anthony disconsolately said before leaning his head back into the chair. As he closed his weary eyes, they felt as heavy as his heart.

Hugo entered the hallway of Number Twelve, Fenner Street. His cheery whistling dwindled as he spied his landlady on the stairs. As he tried to push past, she stubbornly crossed her beefy forearms and blocked his way with her stout form.

'Rent's due and I ain't yet been paid for me other services neither.'

Hugo eyed the blowsy woman with disgust. Now sober, and seeing her with harsh daylight on her gin-bloated countenance, he wasn't sure how

he had stomached making use of her other services. But he had, on more than one occasion when
his depleted funds had kept him incarcerated,
drinking alone in his room at night. Roughly he
shoved her aside and carried on up the stairs.

Once in his dingy chamber, he sat on the edge
of the iron bed and opened the newspaper he had
recently bought. Idly he flicked over pages while
calculating whether a little flattery might prise a
decent free dinner from the old hag.

His eyes drifted over announcements that had
been gazetted, then suddenly whipped back to a
certain paragraph. He read it; reread it avidly,
while shock drained the blood from his face.
Abruptly the paper was scrunched in a fist and
flung at the opposite wall as a string of obsceni-
ties emerged through his teeth.

He paced back and forth over the detritus on the
floor, finally coming to a halt by the window. His
glaring gaze darted fitfully from rooftop to sky to
chimney while inner demons tormented him. Finally he had fought them down, convinced himself
that the die was cast. He had no need to worry: no
other man could have her.

Within ten minutes Hugo Robinson had read-
ied himself to go out. The newspaper was retrieved
and neatly folded and a pocket of his coat sagged

with the weight of cold steel. He quit Fenner Street and, uncaring of the extra expense, hailed a cab to take him to Upper Brook Street.

'I hope I'm not calling at an inconvenient time?'

'Not at all; I've been expecting you.'

Restrained wrath was vibrating his visitor's voice, but left Adam unmoved. Slowly closing one eye, he took aim and sent the ball hurtling bullet-straight into a pocket. He came upright, used the cue as a prop, as he surveyed the man hovering by the door. A flick of Adam's raven head dismissed the butler. 'Do come in,' he urged softly and watched the blond man take a crisp step over the threshold.

'You've been expecting me?' Surprise and suspicion coarsened Hugo's tone. He ventured closer to the magnificent oak-framed billiard table and dropped the newspaper he carried on to green baize. A jerky gesture with a finger indicated *The Times*. 'It's a mistake, then? A joke, perhaps?'

'It's neither,' Adam answered him.

'She is mine, you know that!' The words, strangled by rage, exploded from Hugo's throat. 'You can't steal her from me! I won't let you. I told you about the two of us when you came to Hertford-shire.' This last was a more controlled ejaculation, whiningly accented.

Adam strolled about the table towards him.

Hugo's blue eyes jerked over dispassionate features; he could glean nothing from his expression at all. But there was something about the Marquess's movement that was particularly unnerving: he seemed to be balancing lightly on feet that skimmed polished timber.

'I remember what you said that day. My fiancée has now clarified the matter by telling me about you.' Adam halted so that a mere yard separated them.

During the journey to Upper Brook Street, Hugo had seethed with such boiling frustration he felt sure his chest might explode from the pressure within. The moral high ground was his! Even an autocrat such as Rockingham ought feel guilty for such underhand thievery. He looked anything but ashamed.

Hugo calmed one suspicion worming into his mind: Silver Meredith might be a bold hussy, but it was unthinkable that a young woman would confess to a suitor of Rockingham's stature that she had been tumbled to roll on the ground with her skirts about her ears. He might be licentious, but even Rockingham must baulk at the idea of taking a sullied woman as a wife.

Nevertheless, there remained a niggling anxiety

for having underestimated her. He had not believed Silver canny enough to abandon her rustic swain in favour of a man powerful enough to properly protect her. The fops who had been sniffing about her had posed no threat; they would have scattered the moment he hinted she had already bestowed her favours on him. Perhaps that fool Markham might have tried to linger from chivalry, but he would soon have been sent packing.

Aware of Adam's eyes boring into him, Hugo sauntered to pluck a ball from the baize. With an attempt at sinister insouciance he bowled it forcefully along the table. 'I expect what she has told you about me is that I have been… persistent in my courting of her. And with good reason.'

Adam raised dark brows in studied enquiry.

'It is a delicate matter; suffice to say I have sought to protect her good name by giving her mine before gossip starts. Perhaps you are not aware that she has a reputation for being…shall we say…too wild and impetuous?'

'In what way?' Adam asked smoothly.

Hugo shrugged and spread his hands appealingly. 'You cannot expect a gentleman to divulge such delicate information about a lady.'

'Indeed not; but I'm asking *you*.'

The deliberate insult brought an immediate

scarlet stain to Hugo's cheeks. His eyes narrowed in hatred and a sour smile skewed his mouth. It was time, then, that the prideful Marquess was regaled with a few sordid facts about his betrothed. He longed to tell him of the incident in the woods, and how it had felt to have those silky hips bucking and squirming beneath him. Just a few moments more and he would have taken her virginity. But oddly he was glad he hadn't; the anticipation of possessing her was a constant sensual pulse in his loins that livened every conscious moment. He'd dreamed of her too, and woken more than once with the evidence of his obsession staining the sheets.

Hugo's smile strengthened; soon the smug bastard would be begging him to take such a slut off his hands.

'Very well; but you will be sorry for forcing my hand. Her parents, her sisters, will despise you for it. She will, too, of course, when she finds out how you have bullied the secret from me.'

Adam shrugged careless acceptance of that.

'Earlier this year Silver Meredith ran off with a farmer who lives close to Windrush. They intended to marry at Gretna Green and broke their journey to put up together in a room at the George and Dragon on the Great North Road. Incredibly, she changed her mind about marrying him. They returned home, risking irreparable damage to her reputation by aborting the escapade.' Hugo finished on a triumphant smirk and waited for the outrage that he was sure would follow.

'Anything else?'

Hugo choked an astonished laugh. 'Either you are deaf or you think I am lying.'

'I heard you well enough, and you have the gist of what happened, if not the story in its entirety.'

Hugo's chin sagged towards his chest. 'You knew?'

'Of course I knew. I had a hand in it.'

'What?'

'I was at the tavern. Miss Meredith journeyed there with John Vance to meet me.' Adam smiled thinly at the shocking pallor he had brought to Hugo's face.

'Now I think you are lying,' emerged through Hugo's gritted teeth. 'Do you really expect me to believe that the Marquess of Rockingham would arrange a tryst at such a seedy hole?' he sneered.

'Despicably parsimonious, I know,' Adam agreed with light distaste. 'Nevertheless, it is true. In fact, my lodging there at that time is on record with the authorities. They were called upon to help recover a horse of mine that was stolen from the stables of the George and Dragon.'

Hugo's face became stiff as a mask—he understood the challenge to check the veracity of the information. He swallowed the bile that roared like a furnace in his chest. 'You don't know it all,' he hissed. 'Have you not wondered why I would still want to marry such a strumpet? I tumbled her first. It happened last year…before any of this.' It was an exultant, triumphant declaration. A bark of laughter shook his body and he pointed a quivering, mocking finger. 'She's not told you about the time she begged me to meet her in the woods, has she? She flaunted herself…tempted me with her body. She's a hot wanton, Townsend, and I am destined to finish what I started. Don't you see?'

'I am afraid I don't,' Adam bit out with icy calm. 'In fact, there is no possibility of you attempting to rape my future wife ever again.'

Hugo dragged his fingers through his hair and looked bewildered. 'She was ruined before you bedded her. I had her on her back beneath me months ago, I tell you. Did you not understand what I said?'

'I don't think you understood what I said.' Adam's voice was slow and silky with steel. 'I am going to marry Silver Meredith and you have mistaken your rival. It's not Vance you needed to beat, but me.' Slowly Adam placed the cue on the table edge. 'It's not too late for you to try and remedy matters. I suggest a meeting tomorrow morning at Baker's End. Pemberton will stand for me. If you can find a friend to stand for you, all well and good; if not, buy yourself a second. I'll arrange for a surgeon. Pistols or swords? Fists, if you prefer…'

Hugo stared with ludicrous dismay at the Marquess. He closed his dropped jaw well enough to scornfully snap, 'Only a lunatic would think to fight me for one of my whores.'

A single hard punch finally closed Hugo's mouth and sent him tottering back until he found some support in the billiard table. He hung on to oak with both arms flung out at his sides.

'You'll meet me. Here or there—it makes no difference to me.' Adam's tone was ruthlessly content. 'Make a choice while you still have one.'

Hugo hung his head, started to laugh, his body crumpled and quivering against the squat furniture. He made an effort to straighten up, dusted down his clothes with a negligent hand that suddenly dove into a pocket.

With a feral cry Hugo sprang at Adam with a glint of silver.

Adam lithely sidestepped, but the knife sliced

into his sleeve, nicking skin. With a smooth grab the cue was again in Adam's hand and parrying the next slash of his attacker's dagger.

They fought in silence, parallel to the huge table, each man driving forward, then retreating, lunging and evading with unflinching ferocity. The only sound in the room was laboured breathing and the thud and crack of metal bouncing on wood. Suddenly Hugo stumbled beneath the force of a blow from the cue. Adam took a step aside to allow him to find his feet, hoping he would, for the punishment he had inflicted so far was woefully inadequate to satisfy his lust to avenge Sylvie. The thought of the torment she had endured because of this man was a burning pain that writhed ceaselessly in his gut.

With a smile of satisfaction he watched Hugo drag to his knees with the aid of a table leg. He clung there, head hanging limply as though to steady his reeling senses.

Slyly Hugo lunged upright and, before properly standing, viciously aimed his blade at the Marquess's groin. Adam swivelled out of danger and brought the cue down on Hugo's back, knocking the breath from him so he sprawled flat on the oak boards.

With a groan of exertion Hugo scrabbled his fingers for the knife just beyond his reach. A reptilian slither on his belly brought him close enough to touch the ivory hilt. His howl of pain was followed by a whimpering, 'My God! I think you've broken my hand, Rockingham!'

'It would have been your neck but for the affection and respect I have for your parents.' Adam barely glanced at the limp limb held up for his inspection. He discarded his weapon on to the baize and in a fluid stoop hauled Hugo up by the collar of his jacket. Barely pausing to allow him to properly find his balance, he dragged the younger man to the door of the room and slammed him face front against it.

With a broad hand straddling Hugo's nape, Adam addressed his adversary's sickly profile, pinioned to wood. 'There is no future for you in villainy, Hugo,' he said with almost soothing sympathy. 'You're an enthusiastic rogue, but none the less an amateur. I, on the other hand, have a distinct advantage in that a thousand years of devilry flows in my veins. To make this right, not for you but for Silver Meredith and for your parents, you will do exactly as I say and you will go where I say. Do you understand?'

Hugo shivered his head up and down against timber.

'Good; such cooperation bodes well. Perhaps you may never discover what zealous iniquity has driven the Rockinghams over centuries. Come, I'll give you a ride home and we can discuss things further.'

Chapter Sixteen

'Your leg is less swollen.'

Sir Anthony gave no indication of having discerned the whine of surprise and disappointment in his son's voice. Lounging back in his chair, he stretched out the limb to which Hugo had sullenly referred. 'The Merediths' daughter, Isabel, made me a herbal poultice. Edgar brought it over a day or so ago. In that short time it's eased remarkably the pain and inflammation. I must write and thank the sweet lass.'

Hugo's mouth thinned in bitterness. It was a Meredith woman, again, who was denying him what he deserved. The prospect of soon gaining his birthright was dwindling thanks to the interference of Silver's sister. His father, if not in rude health, appeared more robust than he had in a while.

Cowed by the punishment he'd recently received, Hugo limited his frustration to sniping at the man who had been his nemesis, and who had escorted him home to Rivendale. 'We don't see this fellow in an age, then it seems impossible to avoid him.' It was a discourtesy unmitigated by his sham joviality.

Sir Anthony rebuked his son with a sharp look. He slowly put on his spectacles, then raised his steely head to properly inspect the bruising on Hugo's face, the bandaging on one of his hands. 'It certainly seems that you have found it impossible to avoid someone.' With significance, he transferred his attention to his godson. 'You are very welcome, Adam. As always, it's a pleasure to see you.'

Adam inclined his head in acknowledgement of Sir Anthony's graciousness.

Hugo thrust his fists into his pockets and slid a glance between the striking dark-haired gentleman at ease by the mantelpiece, and the rotund figure of his sire sprawled in a fireside chair.

A worrying perception penetrated Hugo's all-consuming resentment: his father was done with showing him unswerving loyalty because he was his only issue. He realised Sir Anthony had already accepted that his son and heir was guilty of a serious crime and he had no intention of shielding him from justice or retribution. At one time he might have attempted to manipulate his father by petitioning his mother but, today, his father's pitiless cold stare indicated that, if he did, it would be to no avail. Abruptly Hugo turned on a heel and, before quitting the room, muttered, 'I'm packing for a trip.'

A brief silence followed his son's departure and then Sir Anthony asked, 'Do you know how he came by those injuries?'

'Yes; I gave them to him,' Adam replied without a hint of apology or remorse.

Sir Anthony nodded gravely to himself. 'I take it the nature of the matter ought be kept from his mother?'

'Yes.' It was a quietly emphatic affirmative.

Sir Anthony collapsed back in his chair and screwed up his eyes. 'So, I must thank you for disciplining my son and, I imagine, for removing him from town before he made more damnable mischief.' He vigorously swayed his head to and fro in penance before dropping his face into palsied palms. Once a mite recovered, he croaked, 'My apologies for having made it necessary for you to do my dirty work. Had I found the mettle to teach him a few necessary lessons when he was younger, perhaps it might not have come to this.' He extended a silencing hand as Adam sought to demur. 'I know it must be devilry of a serious sort for you to act so, but I don't want to know the sordid details unless I must. Just tell me this: are we to be embroiled in a scandal? Tell me the truth so that I can take whatever steps are necessary to protect Susannah.'

'Hugo has said he will move abroad for the foreseeable future. If you ensure that the promise is honoured, the matter should be contained. I will endeavour to rectify the damage done.'

Sir Anthony struggled to his feet with the help of his cane. He made his way to the window and looked out over the gardens. 'We were so besotted with our baby boy…my cherished heir…that it hardly mattered at the time when the physician told us he would be Susannah's only child.' He twisted about to send a glance at Adam. 'I recall your father despairing of you a decade ago; called you a dissolute rogue.'

Adam grimaced ruefully. 'I can't deny the charge. But in my defence, he was an unusual Rockingham: quite prudish in a way.'

'Unusual indeed!' Sir Anthony roared with laughter. He wiped away a cathartic tear from his eye. 'Would that you had been mine!' he whispered, his voice vibrating with emotion.

* * *

'For a young lady who is engaged to the most handsome bachelor in town, not to mention the most eligible, you do not look as happy as you ought.'

The cup of coffee, which had grown cold while Sylvie stared into its cloudy depths, was removed from her fingers. June placed it on the breakfast table, then leaned across an expanse of mahogany to clasp her sister's hands. 'It is hard to believe that any young lady would reluctantly have Adam Townsend as a husband…but tell me you are not doing this simply out of duty, to please our parents.'

'No. I promise I am not.' The affirmation was accompanied by a small smile.

'Do you love him?' June asked bluntly.

Sylvie looked startled by that question then, with a frown and a solemn tone, answered, 'Yes, I do.'

June appeared more content, even as she chided softly, 'Heavens, Sylvie, you make being in love sound a chore.' She cocked her head and remarked, 'Of course, a marriage does have its ups and downs, but there are quite wonderful advantages.' An adoring eye was cast on her little son, snugly asleep on the sofa. 'I imagine you will receive a fine betrothal ring. Adam has wonderful taste in jewellery.'

Sylvie's smile was wry. 'I'm sure Lady Burdett would say so. I imagine he is a generous man.'

June tutted. 'I thought something was troubling you. Look, my dear, you are to be his *wife*. Besides, I was not referring to any bauble of hers that I had admired. Last year Adam purchased a parure of rubies for his mother. She wore the set at her fiftieth birthday celebration and it seemed magnificent.' Noting that Sylvie looked indifferent to the promise of a splendid jewel, June sighed. 'Oh, very well, if you really want to discuss it, William told me some time ago that Deborah Burdett is no longer Adam's mistress.'

Sylvie suddenly stood up and twitched the cobwebby cloth of her gown. 'She acts as though she is,' she said casually.

'Well she is a fool, for I have observed him look quite annoyed at the way she tries to cling to him.'

Sylvie touched a figurine here, a tulip petal there, her movements in the room mirroring her restive thoughts. In truth, she had hardly given her fiancé's mistress a thought; for other more pressing anxieties were whirling in her mind.

Since that emotional time when she had confessed all to Adam at Vauxhall, and he had renewed his proposal to her, she had seen nothing of him. As he had escorted her back to her sister and brother-in-law, he had gently reassured her that there was no longer a need for her to fret over any of it.

He had said he would send an express to her father, asking for his permission to gazette their engagement. He would also deal with Hugo, he had told her, while soothing fingertips were creating shivery sensations at the nape of her neck.

But when she had gratefully embraced him, and turned her face up for his kiss, he had simply touched cool lips to her brow. Just before they had quit the screening shrubbery, she had again flung her arms about his waist and pressed her body against him. With sweet abandon she had offered up her parted lips, slid them close to his on cool, abrasive skin. But, without even a peck on the cheek in reciprocation, he had gently disengaged himself from her wanton embrace, then taken her back to her sister.

The day that Hugo was due to visit and browbeat her into marrying him had come and gone. Obviously Hugo would have seen, as would the whole *ton*, the announcement of her betrothal to the Marquess of Rockingham. Had Adam done something to ensure he stay away for good? Although Hugo was a cowardly swine, she doubted he would just slink away without attempting to wreak some sort of havoc as a wedding gift.

Her father had obviously quickly replied to Adam's urgent note about their betrothal for the announcement was printed within days. And, in case Sylvie was still dubious of her parents' reaction to the subject of her marriage, she had, that morning, received a lengthy missive from her mother that was conclusive proof of their approval.

In it was described how they could not adequately convey the delight they felt to receive such wonderful news. As soon as her papa was feeling robust they would come to town and properly celebrate the occasion. Arrangements had to be made, her mother had put in bold print: a trousseau, a guest list, food and wine must be chosen... Oh, and by the way, she had added as a postscript, John Vance was making excellent progress.

'Shall we take a drive and see how many green eyes turn your way today?'

June's teasing voice penetrated Sylvie's contemplative mood causing her to wrinkle her nose. The reminder of their shopping trip the previous day was dispiriting—she was not one to relish inspiring envy.

In the fabric emporium they had visited, they had met other young ladies who were in the marriage mart this Season. Despite smiles and correct words, it was quite obvious that several parties were resentful that Miss Silver Meredith had bagged top prize.

Nevertheless she was certainly now sought after by society's *grandes dames*. The Pembertons were popular with the best families and yet June had cheerfully admitted that notables outside their usual circle were bombarding Grove House with cards to every conceivable social occasion. The mantelshelf in her drawing room was decked with expensive parchment, June had said with a little chuckle.

But a more pleasing interlude had occurred when Guy Markham had bounded up to them in Pall Mall. In his inimitable way he had looked sorrowful whilst announcing that he was glad the best man had won. With a lingering touch of his lips to Sylvie's fingertips, he had boldly hinted that he would be privileged to accept the role of chief usher. He had then wheeled away to steer a morose-faced Mr Shepherd in the opposite direction, for he had spied him purposefully approaching.

'I wonder if William has seen Adam at his club, or anywhere?' The question was blurted out in agitation, for Sylvie was growing impatient; she had so much she wanted to say to Adam.

'You are in love!' June archly declared. 'Heavens, Sylvie, it's no time at all since you sprung it all on us. Adam will be back soon enough. I imagine he has a host of things to do now. Perhaps he has gone to make his peace with his mother. I would wager she was in the dark over it all too. I doubt Adam would have told Jake; William has said that their relationship is quite strained.'

Sylvie frowned. 'I got the impression that Adam cares deeply for his brother.'

'He does. It's that minx Jake married that has caused all the problems between them,' June declared pithily before realising it might have been prudent to have kept such information to herself. Briskly she set about tucking a blanket around Jacob.

Sylvie wandered to the window, musing on whether June's remark indicated that Lady Townsend was notoriously unfaithful to her sadly crippled husband.

'Ah! Just the gentleman Sylvie's been longing to see.'

It was an exclamation destined to have Sylvie immediately twisting about in a whisper of muslin.

Noting the blush she had brought to her sister's face, June tried to make amends, yet succeeded only in brightening Sylvie's cheeks. 'That is… umm, Sylvie has missed you these past days.'

William's coach had arrived outside Grove House a few minutes before Adam's curricle and the gentlemen had entered the house together. William understood perfectly the appealing look flashed at him from his wife's large hazel eyes.

'Herbert told me at breakfast that the orange tree has its first fruit. Let's go to the conservatory and take a look in case the blighter drops off by dinnertime.'

His abashed wife gladly took his arm to be whisked from the room.

Sylvie suddenly felt very conscious of her imposing fiancé's presence, and the mild amusement tilting his mouth. She *had* yearned to see him, had dressed elegantly with her platinum hair prettily styled every day just in case he might come. But now she felt shy, and not a little apprehensive. She so wanted all to be right between them, but there were troubling matters to be aired and for her pride's sake it must be done.

'Have you been missing me, sweetheart?'

'Yes, for there are important things I have wanted to say to you.' Sylvie managed to sound quietly composed.

Adam walked closer, carefully observing her expression. 'What sort of things?' he asked lightly.

Following a slight pause, Sylvie started with the grave concern most easily expressed. 'Will Hugo Robinson cause further trouble?'

'You don't need to worry about him any more, Sylvie. He was angry about our betrothal, of course, but, being a commonplace bully, beat a retreat when challenged. I've persuaded him it would be sensible to take another lengthy European tour rather than remain in England and be exposed as a brute and a criminal. I recall his mother once mentioning that he enjoyed his time on the continent when he left university. I think he might sensibly decide to settle overseas until Rivendale is his.'

'I think you must have beaten him to make him agree to that.' It was a sombre statement.

'He came to see me armed with a knife. Once he used it, there was no alternative but for a fight to ensue.'

Sylvie looked startled, then her beautiful violet eyes darted over his athletic form. A note of belligerence betrayed her acute concern. 'Were you hurt? Did he cut you?' she demanded.

'It's nothing. A scratch that required a couple of stitches,' he soothed with a smile.

Sylvie anxiously chewed at her lip before saying, 'Show me; I want to see it.'

Adam took off his jacket and rolled back a fine lawn shirtsleeve.

Sylvie tenderly touched a finger to the jagged wound. 'He is a cowardly beast who deserves punishment, but I shouldn't like his parents brought low over it all.'

'No more would I,' Adam agreed, tidying his dress. 'Sir Anthony and Susannah Robinson are fine people. I have yesterday returned from visiting Rivendale. They seem reconciled to the fact that their son is off on his travels again.' Adam took Sylvie's delicate-boned hands in his and thumbs swept soothingly across satin skin. 'Sir Anthony is no fool; he had suspected that his son was up to no good. It is probably a relief that Hugo will be away from them for a while.'

'Have you news of John?'

Adam flicked his head in assent. 'I briefly visited your parents while I was in the vicinity. Your friend is recovering remarkably well, but it seems he has genuinely little recollection of the incident and does not know who attacked him. I will do whatever is within my power to assist his full recovery. He ought be examined by doctors with special knowledge of head injuries.'

'You are a very good man,' Sylvie said huskily. 'And I am truly grateful to you for all your kind help…'

'But…' Adam prompted quietly, releasing the fingers that courteously fluttered for freedom against his hands.

Sylvie took her lower lip in small teeth and chewed. She tilted her face to look into features of devastating male beauty. 'But I can't marry you.'

'Are you going to tell me why?'

'Yes, of course,' Sylvie agreed politely. 'As well as being too childlike, I am also too proud. I would never marry a man who had proposed from pity or kindness, or even from an admirable sense of chivalry. But thank you in any case for protecting me.'

'That's what you think I feel for you, is it? Pity or kindness or a sense of chivalry?'

Sylvie felt a blush stain her cheeks at the new flinty note to his voice. She was giving him a chance to escape his worthiness, or to tell her that it didn't matter what humiliation Hugo had heaped on her…because he loved her…

But he said no more and she felt her cheeks stinging beneath his unwavering dark regard. Her mouth slanted defiantly. 'I know you don't really want to marry me.'

'And how do you know that?'

'In the same way that I knew two years ago that you *did* want to marry me,' Sylvie promptly answered. 'You don't want to kiss me now—not properly, anyway.'

'I recall recently that you accused me of being shallow for placing too much importance on a kiss.'

Sylvie blushed to the roots of her silky silver hair at that ungallant reminder.

Adam frowned his regret at having disconcerted her. 'If that is all that's worrying you, Sylvie, it's an easily remedied misconception.' His voice was husky with apology, and he approached her with a purposeful step and a sultry glint in his eye.

Sylvie sneaked behind the sofa to evade him. She so wanted to have him embrace her as he had at Vauxhall. She wanted his firm fingers on her skin, the warmth of his mouth on hers. She wanted him to kiss her in the hungry, powerful way he had before she made her awful confession of how Hugo had mistreated her. But most of all she wanted to hear just three simple words.

She felt the heat in her eyes and blinked it away with a light, 'I know you're good at kissing, but you won't fool me. I don't want you to oblige me or soothe my vanity.' She paused and gave him a bright smile. 'I understand. I'm sure that if I were a wealthy marquess, hounded by débutantes, I should not relish having a wife who had been abused by another man. I expect you're disgusted by the thought of kissing me now.'

Adam stuck his hands in his pockets and looked at her with an expression of sheer exasperation. After a moment he turned and walked away.

Sylvie watched his back, hot tears glossing violet eyes before spilling on to ivory skin. She clamped together her lips to stop them forming abject phrases that would not only demean her, but shackle him to his word.

'Perhaps you're right,' Adam said coolly, twisting about by the door. 'If you believe me capable of such hypocrisy and insincerity, it would be as well not to spend the rest of our lives together. I thought in the past month, since you came to London, you had seemed to grow up a little, but I was mistaken. You're still a child if you're prepared to jilt me for just that.'

'It is not just that!' Sylvie cried, indignantly. How dare he act so cool and superior! 'You cannot pretend that *your* character is spotless,' she declared hotly. 'At one time I can't deny that I thought your bad reputation and philandering quite…quite glamorous. But not any more,' she added in a tremulous whisper. 'I was being facetious when I said I should like a husband who was popular with the ladies. In fact, I should like a husband who is mindful of loyalty and fidelity.'

Adam walked a few paces back into the room. 'So, now we have it,' he said quietly. 'Have you been discussing my family with June? Perhaps my sister-in-law, in particular, has been a topic of conversation. Is that it?'

Sylvie frowned in bewilderment but admitted honestly, 'We did mention her earlier. I now know that you and Jake are not close because of *that minx.*'

Adam smiled grimly. 'Your sister has a nice way with understatement. My brother hates me because of that minx. So, the truth is you're accusing me of feeling disgust for you when, in fact, the reverse is true. You're blaming me for not wanting to marry you when it's you who wants to be free. Did you deliberately use me to rid you of Hugo Robinson so the way was left clear for you to take up again with your farmer?'

'No!' Sylvie gasped.

Adam barely heard the denial for the bitter laugh that was grazing his throat. 'I may not be able to fool you,' he ground out, 'but you certainly managed to make a monkey out of me.'

'It's not like that!' Sylvie sobbed in desperation, but the door slamming as Adam quit the room made useless the rest of her attempt to explain.

Chapter Seventeen

Sylvie twitched aside velvet and watched her mother being assisted by a servant into the coach. June followed next, ascending with her husband's help. Her father and William then took their places in the vehicle that was to convey them to Deborah Burdett's *musicale*.

Just before the driver set the fine horses to a trot, Gloria Meredith's wan countenance appeared at a carriage window. She peered up at her daughter's lighted casement. A guilty sob cluttered Sylvie's throat as she noticed tears glistening on her mother's cheeks.

Dropping the heavy curtain back into place, Sylvie closed her eyes for the angry words she had suffered listening to that very afternoon were again battering her aching head.

You must come with us this evening! The Marquess is sure to attend Lady Burdett's concert. Find an opportunity to be private with him and apologise. He has not yet approached your papa to discuss formally breaking the betrothal. All is not yet lost. Oh, I cannot believe you have done this! What is the matter with you, girl? Are you determined to shame us all with your selfish shenanigans?

Sylvie had miserably endured the censure, wishing there was some way she could tell her mother that it was not *all* her fault. But to explain the rift between Adam and her would necessitate revealing the whole sordid tale of Hugo's abuse, and Adam's knowledge of it. She had thus mumbled about misunderstandings that had sprung up between them, and pleaded a migraine as an excuse to going out.

Sylvie was not intimidated by the thought of being a guest of Adam's paramour. She had an instinct that Deborah Burdett posed no real threat. If Adam loved the young widow, surely he would by now have made her his wife.

Her desire to remain at home sprang from another reason entirely. Her mother's plaintive hope that all was not yet lost had echoed her own wistful thoughts.

Although Adam and she had been at loggerheads again, Sylvie had sensed that he had felt more hurt than angry… just as she had. A woman's intuition also told her he yearned for reassurance from her as much as she craved it from him.

He had an annoying habit of storming off during an argument before she could make a proper explanation, or insist that he do so. A small smile slanted her soft lips as she realised that the Marquess of Rockingham was no longer the stranger he once was. She was coming to understand him quite well. He would eventually get used to the idea of her challenging him, even if he was a wealthy peer of the realm and fawned over by all and sundry.

Perhaps, when Adam discovered that she was languishing alone at Grove House, he might slip away from the *musicale* and come to see her. It was right *he* should be the one to make a conciliatory move. She had generously offered to give him back his freedom. In return, he had accused her of using him in a mercenary way, and of trying to make a fool of him. She would never act so meanly. She loved him utterly. But she would not again grovel as she had when she had chased him to Lady Burdett's door, then proposed to him in the hackney cab.

Sylvie glanced at the clock and, in irritation, twirled a ringlet about a finger. She watched the stubby brass hand jump to the hour and strike nine of the clock. Her lips compressed. Her puerile hope that her fiancé might leave his mistress's side, to come and try to put things right between them, had withered to ashes. Had she misjudged even that aspect of his character? Far from being inconsequential, perhaps Deborah Burdett could lure Adam with a crooked finger.

During the last two hours Sylvie had flicked through fashion journals, and stitched a whole pansy on to a handkerchief that had then been crumpled and flung on to the floor. She had even attempted reading her new novel from the circulating library.

The Madeira decanter arrested her furiously flitting glance. When her mother was exasperated with her father, she often took a little comfort from it. Well, she was woman enough to have a fiancé, and to be frustrated by the dratted man. Defiantly she poured a small amount into a glass, then took a gulp. She choked as the stinging warmth clung to her throat, but determinedly took another careful sip.

After a few mellow moments she decided it would not hurt to be generous, swallow her pride, and pen him a note. In it she would admit that John had never been more to her than a cherished friend. Phrases began to merge fluently in her mind. A little more Madeira was sloshed into her glass and she took it with her to settle at the writing desk in the library.

He would be impressed by her great sacrifice, Sylvie decided as she got unsteadily into the hackney cab. Whilst he was enjoying himself—being popular with the ladies, no doubt—she had sneaked out of Grove House and was again risking her reputation to deliver a *billet doux* to her beloved.

With a sigh, she flopped back into the squabs to ponder on her wonderfully intrepid nature, while her hands cupped her rosy cheeks to try to cool their inebriated flush.

Before quitting the house, and caught up in the spirit of the adventure, she had donned her shabbiest cloak, reasoning that a modestly dressed woman out alone in the evening, perhaps on an errand, would attract less attention than would a fashionable young lady. An enveloping hood of dun-coloured cloth was carefully tweaked, to shield her delicate fair features, before she took a peek out of the cab window into the looming gloom.

Once on the pavement in Upper Brook Street, misty evening air, and the forbidding façade of the Marquess of Rockingham's magnificent townhouse, combined to dampen her Dutch courage. The fog in her head was dispersing and sobering thoughts had tied her stomach in knots. Far from feeling heroic, Sylvie now felt foolish and not a little apprehensive. She realised that her lone excursion to Mayfair had been reckless and would never have been undertaken but for her attempt to drown her sorrows in a decanter of Madeira.

A couple, strolling arm in arm, were approaching and she huddled against the railing. She busily scanned the note she had written, as though checking an address. A sliding peek from beneath her hood reassured her that her drab figure received barely a glance as they swept by.

Sylvie peered about. She had come this far, if she turned tail without even delivering the letter she had written, it would all be a squandered effort. With an inspiriting breath, she quashed her misgivings and darted up steep stone steps to rap on an enormous door.

Almost immediately a footman appeared, resplendent in a uniform heavily adorned with gold frogging. Before Sylvie could utter a word he winked at her and hissed, 'Should've used the other door! Quick, in you come before Mr Bartholomew gets wind of how late it is. You're lucky he's been taken poorly. Gumboil the size of an egg, he has.' The gregarious young man blew out one cheek to demonstrate the butler's affliction.

Sylvie simply proffered her parchment, too nervous to loiter and to attempt to comprehend that strange greeting. 'Would you make sure that this is delivered?'

'You'll have to give your character to Mr Bartholomew,' the servant interrupted her, rejecting her precious note. 'Mrs Hooper 'ud usually take it, she's the housekeeper, as you'd know, but she ain't here today; gone off to a funeral she has.'

'No…please, listen, you don't understand…'

Suddenly the footman grabbed one of her arms and hauled her over the threshold. 'Come in, fer Gawd's sake,' he rasped in exasperation while straightening his wig, knocked askew by the exertion. 'I can't help you less'n you help yourself. Bartholomew's a stickler fer punctuality. If he comes by, he'll know you didn't make a show till now. And once Mrs Hooper gets wind of it all, you won't get taken on. You'll be back down them steps.'

Sylvie shook herself free, her emotions veering between hysteria and indignation. Disguising oneself in common attire was one thing, being mistaken for a hired hand was something else entirely.

'I'm Hobson,' the grinning footman told her as

he angled his head to see beneath her hood. 'Don't be shy; let's have a good look at you.' He made to flick the hood away from her blonde hair.

Sylvie forcefully slapped away his impertinent hand.

'Would someone care to explain to me just what is going on?'

A stunned silence was finally broken by slow footfalls echoing eerily on the stone flags.

Sylvie had immediately tensed rigid on recognising that husky drawl. She speared a glance at the footman; his hand had petrified in space, in the exact position to which she had knocked it.

A sumptuous chandelier was flickering a mellow glow over alabaster surfaces. Between shadows she could properly observe Hobson's features. He was about her age, and he looked terrified. His complexion had whitened and his throat was ceaselessly bobbing. Sylvie guessed that it was probably the first time the young footman had been directly addressed by the master of the house.

'Mr Bartholomew's got a gumboil, my lord,' Hobson croaked. 'Tindall's got the bellyache, or he'd be on duty…as for Mrs Hooper—'

'Spare me the rest of the staff's misfortune.' It was an indolent appeal as the Marquess of Rockingham propped his rugged physique against graceful marble. 'I understand why you opened the door. What I want to know is, what have you done to make this woman hit you? Who is she?'

'I done nothing, honest, m'lord,' Hobson spluttered earnestly. 'Just arst her to come in so's I could close the door. She's Sandra Riley, the new girl as was expected this morning. Mrs Hooper deals with females, but she's gone to a funeral.'

Sylvie took a deep breath. She could cravenly scamper out of the house, or she could reveal her identity, and spare Hobson suffering for having tried to save Sandra Riley her job. Remotely, she wondered where that young woman had got to. With a gulp of inspiriting breath she swung about and shook back the hood from her face. Her sculpted chin immediately tilted to a proud angle and violet eyes challenged the man who might or might not still be her fiancé.

If he was astonished to see her—a reaction to which she allowed he had every right—he was admirably concealing it. Perhaps alcohol had dulled his senses much in the same way as previously it had hers. He had obviously been drinking: the liquor glass oscillating between a thumb and forefinger was testament to that. He had obviously been at his ease too: white shirtsleeves rolled back to display sinewy tanned forearms indicated he'd not expected company.

'Sandra Riley…you take the most appalling risks with your reputation, my dear.'

'I know. But I did tell you that acting shamelessly seems to be my way,' Sylvie countered in a voice that was slightly unsteady. Obliquely she was aware of Hobson goggling at her, his jaw slackening, as he struggled to comprehend the odd discourse between his illustrious master and the new maid.

In a show of bravado, Sylvie took a few unsteady steps into the cool white hallway. 'I was sure you would be attending Lady Burdett's *musicale*. I intended delivering you a letter whilst you were out.'

Adam extended a languid hand, palm up, while the other brought the brandy to his mouth.

Sylvie's fingers tightened on the parchment. 'No; it doesn't matter, now,' she murmured. 'It was just another mistake I made, that's all.' The note was slipped out of sight in a pocket of her shabby cloak. 'I'm sorry to have bothered you.' She gracefully swept back to the door. 'Let me out, please.' It was a polite request, but a hand was already on the cumbersome handle. If Hobson tarried too long, she would perform the office herself.

Hobson stared nervously at his master for instruction. An abrupt flick of Adam's dark head was all it took for the footman to gladly take rapid paces towards the baize door that led below stairs.

On realising she was not about to gain her freedom, Sylvie twisted about to watch Hobson disappear from view, and Adam deposit his glass on a console table on his way towards her. Quickly she attended, double-handed, to the door herself. The heavy oak groaned open a few inches, only to be pressed shut again by dark fingers leaning on the panel above her head.

'Let me out!'

'No.'

'Let me out!' Sylvie demanded in a shrill whisper as dew darkened her lashes.

'Why are you crying?' Adam asked softly as he curbed her attempts to flee from him by imprisoning her slender figure between two muscular brown arms.

Sylvie dashed away the wet. 'I'm not! Well, I am, but only because I'm angry.'

'At me?'

'A little,' she honestly admitted with a small sniffle. 'But mostly I'm angry at myself.'

'Why?'

'*Why?*' Sylvie mimicked with a scornful sob.

'Because I have again acted foolishly! Twice now I have humbled myself to try and make things right between us. No more! It's *your* place to woo *me*.'

'I know it is, so I can't even plead woeful ignorance about such things,' he said with gentle irony.

'You could plead woeful arrogance,' Sylvie stormed in a watery choke.

'True,' the Marquess indulgently concurred. 'It's not a serious disorder, sweetheart. I'm confident you have a cure for it.'

Adam's eyes roved her delicately beautiful countenance, luxuriating in the gift of her presence. Despite her furious embarrassment at being caught in his home, the bold elevation to her chin was undiminished.

'It's brave of you to come here to put things right between us…and foolish, but then every courageous act is essentially a risk.' He lightly gathered on to a fingertip a tear that had rolled to her mouth. 'You put me to shame—I nearly came to you this afternoon, but my damnable pride stopped me. Now you are here, I want you to stay, so I can talk to you…and woo you.'

Sylvie swerved glossy eyes to his, her face burning beneath the dark fiery heat between his lashes. He dipped his head slightly and, for a tantalising moment, she was sure he would kiss her.

He was close enough for her to recognise the sweet scent of alcohol on his breath. She responded to his magnetism, her body swaying towards his. Abruptly he straightened, as though recalling they were in full view of any servants who might be tempted to spy on them. 'Will you stay with me?' he pleaded hoarsely.

Sylvie gave a small nod. She cleared her throat, said briskly, 'I mustn't tarry long, of course, for I will be missed and then chaos will ensue.'

'Come; there's a small library just across the hallway.' Adam took her arm and gently urged her away from the door. 'I was in there, sitting by the fire, when you arrived.'

Once inside the oak-panelled room Adam led Sylvie towards a seat by the glowing grate. He took up position close by, with a foot propped against the fender. 'What made you so sure I'd be at Lady Burdett's?'

Sylvie sensed his sole purpose in mentioning that woman was to establish between them her role in his life. She bluntly obliged him, for candour was all she would now deal in. 'She is known to be your mistress. Why would you not attend her concert?'

'Deborah is a friend now, nothing more. Much in the same way that I hope John Vance is a friend now…and nothing more.'

'John has always been simply a friend,' Sylvie said huskily. 'I love him, but not…not with romantic passion. When we stayed at the George and Dragon, he treated me with respect and consideration. We have kissed once or twice, but he has never attempted to seduce me. I have always trusted him. And I would far sooner have had him for my husband than Hugo Robinson.'

'I'm very grateful to him for caring so well for you,' Adam said gruffly. 'I owe him a great deal.'

'You're not jealous of him any more?' Sylvie asked, her eyes flicking up to his face.

Adam gave her a lop-sided smile, then looked down a little self-consciously. He forcefully nudged the fender with the toe of a boot. 'I probably am, for you do love him.'

Sylvie slowly rose from her chair and approached him by the fire. She stood before him, her silver hair burnished to auburn by flickering embers. Suddenly she tipped up her chin and whispered shyly, 'You're much older than me so you ought say it first. I expect you've done so before.'

Adam raised a hand that vibrated slightly. With infinite tenderness it slid to cup a cheek, bringing her face closer to his. 'I love you, Silver Meredith. You soothe my soul and improve my character and I think my body might eventually benefit

too. But you're wrong. I've never said it before…
or even felt remotely tempted to do so.'

Sylvie suddenly plunged her arms about his
waist and hugged him. 'And I love you with romance and passion and all my heart.'

Adam smiled indulgently at her inexperienced
embrace. His fingers forked into her silken hair,
cradling her scalp against his chest. 'I haven't yet
said all I must, Sylvie. I could have told you weeks
ago that I loved you, but…I've been worried that
when you find out more about me, you might despise me. You don't know exactly why my brother
hates me, do you?'

Sylvie shook her head, sending silver to ripple
about her gracefully solemn features. 'Does it matter?' she whispered.

'Yes, it matters,' Adam said hoarsely while his
fingertips skimmed satin skin at the nape of her
neck. Abruptly he held her a little way from him;
then, as though it was an effort to relinquish contact, he suddenly snatched his hands to his sides.
'Yesterday you described me as a good man. It's
not true, Sylvie. I'm a Rockingham with a full
quota of my family's vices. In my life I've drunk,
gambled and fornicated far too much because I
saw no reason to deny myself a solitary thing.' He
paused and momentarily closed his eyes to block

the sight of her pure, trusting gaze. 'Theresa was my mistress before she was Jake's wife. My brother hates me because she was my mistress again after they married.'

Sylvie continued to wordlessly gaze at him, for disbelief had dried her mouth. Eventually she blinked rapidly and gasped, 'You made a cuckold of your own brother?'

Adam straightened his shoulders, drove his hands into his pockets. A slightly defensive set to his mouth betrayed that he feared she might now voice her disgust. After a moment he said, 'They had been married about a year when Theresa came to see me one evening to tell me that Jake had been mortally injured fighting on the Peninsula. I honestly believed he had died, but that's a paltry excuse. The least I should have done was respectfully bury him before bedding his widow. I shan't pretend there was any decent emotion involved in our coupling. I can't even claim we sought mutual comfort over our loss, it was nothing…just lust.'

Sylvie stared at him as the strength of his self-loathing contorted his features. She ought feel similar abhorrence, she knew that, but the logic perished beneath an overwhelming need to comfort him. 'It doesn't make you wicked, Adam…not really,' Sylvie said gently. 'Not if you truly believed your brother was dead. We are none of us perfect and will fail at times. I have suffered guilty feelings too…so many…and most—no, all, I think—sprang from acting selfishly and hurting people I love.' She paused, sent him a grave look. 'What happened when you found out Jake was alive? Was Theresa still your mistress?'

'No! I finished with her and cravenly hoped Jake would not find out,' he admitted.

'But he heard the gossip?'

'Theresa told him. She was repelled by Jake's disfigurement. She wanted me to provide her with her own residence and my protection. She still does. She'd leave him tomorrow for that.'

'That's why you followed her to the George and Dragon and took her home. You are still trying to make amends for betraying Jake.'

Adam simply nodded. 'It's not the first time I've done so, but it is the last.'

'And those Rockingham vices, are they all in your past?' Sylvie's voice was sweet yet firm.

'I suspect that depends on whether you agree to marry me, Sylvie. Without you bullying me to behave, I'm sure to relapse, you know.'

A smile started to curve Sylvie's soft mouth, but it was swiftly curbed. 'Don't joke!' she pleaded. 'I meant what I said about wanting a husband who is mindful of loyalty and fidelity, for otherwise…our love would seem so…so pointless.'

'Since I saw you at the George and Dragon I've thought about you constantly. I've changed what I do…how I live, simply to be close to you. Much as I hoped to see my future godson, I came to Hertfordshire looking for you, not Jacob.' Adam paused, looked rather diffident. 'When I believed you married to John Vance I was thinking of ways I could persuade you to become my mistress. I loved and wanted you when you were sixteen, but was reluctant to admit as much even to myself. How could an innocent, angelic child have such power over me? But you did. You're all I want, Sylvie, you must know that.'

His frustrated need for her coarsened his voice and in response Sylvie felt her body weaken, become pliant. 'You don't mind about what Hugo did to me?'

'Of course I mind,' he groaned. 'I want to kill the bastard for what he did to you, not send him on a jaunt abroad. Your first experience of intimacy between a man and a woman should have been pleasurable, something to cherish. Instead he made it a loathsome ordeal. I can't ever forgive him for that, Sylvie,' Adam said hoarsely, his distress coating glitter on his dark eyes.

As Sylvie came to him, put out her hands to comfort him, he clasped those questing fingers, brought them to his lips. Reverentially he saluted each one. 'Listen to me and believe utterly what I say. Hugo Robinson is a disgrace to humanity. He is a brute and a coward who is not fit to touch the ground you step upon. And had I known you truly wanted me to kiss you—not from gratitude for rescuing you from that devil, but from love and desire—then we would not have emerged from those bushes for some hours.'

Sylvie gazed up into dark eyes that were at one and the same time adoring and devouring. Bursting with love for him, Sylvie shot her arms out to hug him, but was caught at the wrists in a tender grip. Adam pulled her against his solid body, guided her slender arms about his neck, and locked her fingers at his nape. 'Like that, Sylvie,' he whispered against her mouth. 'I like it better like that,' he tutored her before his mouth moulded against hers, softly bestowing her sensual reward.

Chapter Eighteen

'I must go!'

The declaration emerged as a sob of frustration.

'Not yet, Sylvie,' Adam growled out the plea.

Sylvie sighed blissfully, ceding gratefully to his dominance as she was pressed back into the hide sofa and seduced with another potent kiss. She relaxed beneath him with a sensual undulation that demanded a dark hand resume lavishing slow caresses on her pearly flesh.

His mouth relinquished her pulsing lips, slid a moist trail to breasts peeking over lace. Sylvie arched her back and panted her delight into the shadowy atmosphere as his tongue leisurely flicked, circled, relentlessly teased. She wriggled her legs free of her hampering skirts then snaked silken calves about the brawny strength of his. With primitive instinct she thrust her hips into contact with his pelvis.

Adam gave a ragged groan and protected the ache in his breeches by pinning her against the cushions with tender hands. He gazed down in triumph and wonderment at her languorous expression, her glazed eyes barely open, her swollen mouth provocatively wide. Peace and contentment shuddered through him as he laid his head down in the cosy nook by her shoulder. 'I was terrified that Hugo's depravity had made you consider all men to be revolting brutes. I wondered if you would ever want me to kiss and caress you, let alone do more…'

Sylvie turned her face, blindly sensed where his mouth was to merge their skin, touch her tongue to his, in the delicately erotic way he had shown her. 'I never imagined it could be marvellous like this,' she whispered shyly as her lashes fluttered up.

Adam raised himself on an elbow, possessively curving his body over hers. He smoothed back silver tresses from febrile ivory skin. 'You'll be my wife before we do more than this, I swear.'

'I think I might like to do more than this,' Sylvie murmured teasingly, then earnestly added, 'I do trust you, Adam.'

Adam slid a finger over her scarlet, slick lips. 'I know you do, sweetheart. But our first time should be special. You deserve to have a proper wedding night with a fine feather bed, and silk sheets and champagne.'

Sylvie smiled. 'I don't mind a leather sofa, it is comfortable, and I had some Madeira before I left home. Had I not, I wouldn't have found the courage to come here at all.' As he dipped his head to kiss her, she bashfully averted her face. 'I suppose I must be an incurable wanton to speak so.'

'I'm optimistic that you might be,' Adam said with such wicked amusement in his eyes and voice that she blushed and turned away. 'Don't be shy, Sylvie,' he murmured tenderly, shifting her back against him. 'A woman could bestow no sweeter gift on the man who loves her than to match his passion.'

Sylvie smiled against skin like musky satin, revelling in the feeling that molten honey circulated in her veins. She held aloft her left hand to admire the fine gift *she* had received. The magnificent jewel he had slipped on to her betrothal finger felt cool and heavy.

An hour or more ago Adam had led her to the sofa and gone down on not one, but both bended knees to present her engagement ring. It was by responding so generously to his wry humility, and the formal token of their love, that her clothing had got in such disarray. She rotated her hand this way and that until the huge oval diamond caught the glow from the grate and changed colour.

Sylvie gazed with quiet devotion at Adam, not sparing him, until his eyelids drooped and he smiled in that rueful way he had. Abruptly she coiled her arms about his waist and held him tightly. 'I don't want to go home. I want to stay with you.'

'Are you sure?' he asked after a lengthy pause.

Sylvie nodded against his naked ribs, exposed some while ago when his snowy shirt had, at some point during their passion, lost half its buttons. 'Do you want me to go home?'

'No.'

'This is my home now?'

'Yes.'

Sylvie contentedly burrowed her head more comfortably against a muscled torso.

Adam threaded a hand into a tangle of platinum hair, gently tilting her face up to his. 'You know what this means, don't you, Sylvie?'

Sylvie wrinkled her nose. 'A scandal, I suppose.'

Adam choked a laugh and shifted her properly on top of him, close enough for a swift, hard kiss. 'Indeed it will be if tonight we don't elope.'

Epilogue

Gloria Meredith lifted her eyes from her embroidery to quietly appreciate the sunbeams slanting low across the rose trellis in the garden. The curtain close to her chair stirred, wafting midsummer scent into the sitting room. As a blackbird started to sweetly serenade sunset, a feeling of serenity eased her back against the cushions. Very soon the vivid streaks of colour on the horizon would fade and darkling shadows would stalk the lawns to steal beauty from the flowers.

A guttural noise drew her attention from pastoral perfection back into the sitting room. She cast a fond look at her husband dozing by the fireside. Another rumbling snore shook Edgar's chest, seeming to jerk him back to consciousness. He clasped the velvet arms in which he reposed and, blinking rapidly, darted a glance at his wife. On seeing Gloria watching him, he gave a little cough and grabbed the poker. Busily he stirred to life the logs in the grate even though the room was warm enough.

With a private smile Gloria picked up her embroidery and stitched, pondering idly on male idiosyncrasy. She really didn't mind if he took a snooze whilst she sat with him, but she recalled her own papa had been the same. He would slump with an open book on his lap for an hour or more rather than reveal he had been caught with his defences down.

'Windrush is quiet without our Sylvie,' Gloria said conversationally as her needle weaved.

'Indeed.' It was a dry response.

'It was bad of her to elope like that,' Gloria said with a smile, pulling the thread tight. 'I had plans for a grand society wedding.'

Edgar sent his wife an ironic look. 'I imagine she guessed as much and that's why she took off.' He chuckled and waved away her objection. 'Did you really think that our Sylvie would act so decorous?'

'Of course! Every girl wants to be a princess on her wedding day. That Adam Townsend was to blame, if you ask me.' Gloria's smile was proud as she reflected on her new son-in-law. 'The rogue could not wait for it all to be arranged. I could tell that time when he visited us at Windrush to see baby Jacob that he couldn't keep his eyes from her. I doubt his hands would prove easier to control. He does not strike me as a fellow much acquainted with self-denial.'

Edgar grunted a laugh. 'I'd say you're right about that, my dear. Our Sylvie is an exquisite beauty. And Adam is a definite Rockingham. But he's met his match.'

'Oh, yes.' Gloria's lips formed a satisfied moue. She cocked her head and gazed contentedly into space. 'We are very fortunate, you know. A marchioness, a countess—and another in waiting, for Étienne is due to inherit at any time—and a fine lady. Who would not be immensely proud of such daughters, and the fine gentlemen they have brought into our family? And we have a clutch of the most beautiful grandchildren. How does that make you feel, Mr Meredith?'

'Elated…and exhausted,' Edgar said drolly as he settled his clasped hands on his lap. 'And how do you feel, Mrs Meredith?'

'Exactly the same,' Gloria said. 'Heaven knows there was many a time fraught with anxiety, but I'd gladly do it all again.'

'You would?' Edgar slowly pushed himself out

of his chair and approached his wife with a twinkle in his eye. He took her small, freckled hands into his, easing her to her feet. A tender kiss on her brow welcomed her close. 'Well, I'm game if you are, my dear. It's a long time since we had an early night…'

* * * * *

MILLS & BOON®

Live the emotion

Historical
romance™

ONE STARRY CHRISTMAS

STORMWALKER'S WOMAN *by Carolyn Davidson*

Jesse Stormwalker knew associating with Molly Thompson
could ruin the young widow's reputation, but he sensed that
only he could mend her broken spirit. Jesse hoped that the
miracle of Christmas would make all things possible...

HOME FOR CHRISTMAS *by Carol Finch*

When bounty hunter Seth Gresham brought his friend's
estranged daughter home for Christmas, he never suspected
that both of them had been had. Once Olivia discovered her
father wasn't dying – just matchmaking – would Seth's love
make her stay?

HARK THE HARRIED ANGELS *by Lynna Banning*

Adam Garnett thought he had nothing to offer Irina Likov
– until meddlesome strangers intervened. Now his decision
to give Irina a Christmas she'll remember gives Adam the
greatest gift of all...

CONQUEST BRIDE *by Meriel Fuller*

Baron Varin de Montaigu is a soldier for King William.
By royal decree he must uncover a plot to overthrow the
King – and he is suspicious of everyone. Lady Eadita of
Thunorslege hates the Normans with all her heart, and
wants them out of her country. Varin is certain she is
plotting, and is intent on keeping her close...

On sale 4th November 2005

*Available at most branches of WHSmith, Tesco, ASDA,
Borders, Eason, Sainsbury's and most bookshops*

Visit www.millsandboon.co.uk

1005/04b

MILLS & BOON®

Live the emotion

Historical
romance™

A REPUTABLE RAKE *by Diane Gaston*

Cyprian Sloane's reputation is of the very worst.
Gambler, smuggler, rake and spy, he faces the greatest
challenge of all – respectability! But then he meets
Morgana Hart, whose caring nature thrusts her into the
company of ladies of the night and risks a scandal that
will destroy them both. Is there a way for the rake to
save them?

PRINCESS OF FORTUNE
by Miranda Jarrett

When an exiled princess becomes too much for her hosts
to handle, Captain Lord Thomas Greaves is called in.
Playing nursemaid to a pampered beauty isn't exactly
how he wants to serve his country, and he counts the
days until he can return to sea. The homesick Isabella is
imperious and difficult – but she can't deny her attraction
to her handsome bodyguard…

On sale 4th November 2005

Available at most branches of WHSmith, Tesco, ASDA,
Borders, Eason, Sainsbury's and most bookshops

Visit www.millsandboon.co.uk

MILLS & BOON®

The *Regency*

LORDS & LADIES
COLLECTION

Two glittering Regency
love affairs in every book

1st July 2005	The Larkswood Legacy *by Nicola Cornick* & The Neglectful Guardian *by Anne Ashley*
5th August 2005	My Lady's Prisoner *by Ann Elizabeth Cree* & Miss Harcourt's Dilemma *by Anne Ashley*
2nd September 2005	Lady Clairval's Marriage *by Paula Marshall* & The Passionate Friends *by Meg Alexander*
7th October 2005	A Scandalous Lady *by Francesca Shaw* & The Gentleman's Demand *by Meg Alexander*
4th November 2005	A Poor Relation *by Joanna Maitland* & The Silver Squire *by Mary Brendan*
2nd December 2005	Mistress or Marriage? *by Elizabeth Rolls* & A Roguish Gentleman *by Mary Brendan*

Available at most branches of WH Smith, Tesco, ASDA, Martins, Borders,
Eason, Sainsbury's and all good paperback bookshops.

REG/L&L/LIST

1105/108/MB143

Step back in time to the American West...

...where passions run deep and love lasts forever.

Introducing three captivating stories
from bestselling authors

SUSAN MALLERY
BRONWYN WILLIAMS
& CAROLYN DAVIDSON

*Featuring the Kincaid brothers – three
passionate, determined men – and the women
they love in Whitehorn, Montana.*

On sale 4th November 2005

*Available at most branches of WHSmith, Tesco, ASDA,
Borders, Eason, Sainsbury's and most bookshops*

MILLS & BOON®

Live the emotion

Look out for next month's
Super Historical Romance

A USEFUL AFFAIR
by Stella Cameron

The Marquis of Granville's deadly efficiency makes him invaluable to the Crown. But killing is too good for Bernard Leggit, the wealthy and corrupt merchant responsible for murdering two people Granville held dear. He has a better plan – seduce the old man's young wife, Hattie, then let society know about their affair.

Granville can almost smell his revenge, but his unexpected desire for Hattie – so obviously willing to do almost anything to escape her odious husband – risks putting both of their lives in danger . . .

'Cameron blends sensuality, mystery, danger and some funny moments in this satisfying tale of love.'
—*Romantic Times* on *Testing Miss Toogood*

On sale Friday 4th November 2005

Available at most branches of WHSmith, Tesco, ASDA, Borders, Eason, Sainsbury's and most bookshops

www.millsandboon.co.uk

researching the cure

The facts you need to know:

- **One woman in nine** in the United Kingdom will develop breast cancer during her lifetime.

- Each year **40,700** women are newly diagnosed with breast cancer and around **12,800** women will die from the disease. However, survival rates are improving, with on average 77 per cent of women still alive five years later.

- **Men can also suffer from breast cancer**, although currently they make up less than one per cent of all new cases of the disease.

Britain has one of the highest breast cancer death rates in the world. Breast Cancer Campaign wants to understand why and do something about it. Statistics cannot begin to describe the impact that breast cancer has on the lives of those women who are affected by it and on their families and friends.

BCC/AD b

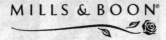

MILLS & BOON®

During the month of October Harlequin Mills & Boon will donate 10p from the sale of every Modern Romance™ series book to help Breast Cancer Campaign in *researching the cure.*

Breast Cancer Campaign's scientific projects look at improving diagnosis and treatment of breast cancer, better understanding how it develops and ultimately either curing the disease or preventing it.

Do your part to help

Visit <u>www.breastcancercampaign.org</u>

And make a donation today.

researching the cure

Breast Cancer Campaign is a company limited by guarantee registered in England and Wales. Company No. 05074725. Charity registration No. 299758.
Breast Cancer Campaign, Clifton Centre,110 Clifton Street, London EC2A 4HT.
Tel: 020 7749 3700 Fax: 020 7749 3701 www.breastcancercampaign.org

2 FREE

BOOKS AND A SURPRISE GIFT!

We would like to take this opportunity to thank you for reading this Mills & Boon® book by offering you the chance to take TWO more specially selected titles from the Historical Romance™ series absolutely FREE! We're also making this offer to introduce you to the benefits of the Reader Service™—

- ★ FREE home delivery
- ★ FREE gifts and competitions
- ★ FREE monthly Newsletter
- ★ Exclusive Reader Service offers
- ★ Books available before they're in the shops

Accepting these FREE books and gift places you under no obligation to buy, you may cancel at any time, even after receiving your free shipment. Simply complete your details below and return the entire page to the address below. You don't even need a stamp!

YES! Please send me 2 free Historical Romance books and a surprise gift. I understand that unless you hear from me, I will receive 4 superb new titles every month for just £3.65 each, postage and packing free. I am under no obligation to purchase any books and may cancel my subscription at any time. The free books and gift will be mine to keep in any case.

H5ZED

Ms/Mrs/Miss/Mr ....Initials ....
BLOCK CAPITALS PLEASE

Surname ....

Address ....

....

....Postcode..

Send this whole page to:
UK: FREEPOST CN81, Croydon, CR9 3WZ

Offer valid in UK only and is not available to current Reader service subscribers to this series. Overseas and Eire please write for details. We reserve the right to refuse an application and applicants must be aged 18 years or over. Only one application per household. Terms and prices subject to change without notice. Offer expires 31st January 2006. As a result of this application, you may receive offers from Harlequin Mills & Boon and other carefully selected companies. If you would prefer not to share in this opportunity please write to The Data Manager, PO Box 676, Richmond, TW9 1WU.

Mills & Boon® is a registered trademark owned by Harlequin Mills & Boon Limited.
Historical Romance™ is being used as a trademark. The Reader Service™ is being used as a trademark.